BOOK TWO

MINDSPACE

CONSPIRACY

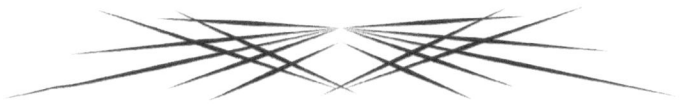

A K DUBOFF

Published by Dawnrunner Press
Cover Copyright © 2021 A.K. DuBoff

ISBN-10: 1954344120
ISBN-13: 978-1954344129
Copyright Registration Number: TX0008730706

0 9 8 7 6 5 4 3

Produced in the United States of America

TABLE OF CONTENTS

KEY TERMS, CAST & LOCATIONS

KEY TERMS

Taran – The race of all people in the Taran Empire; synonymous with human

Tararian Guard – The primary military force for the Taran Empire

Jump – Faster-than-light travel through subspace

Beacon Network – The navigation method for subspace jumps, maintained by SiNavTech

High Dynasties – The seven ruling families of the Taran Empire, collectively a governing council

Tararian Selective Service (TSS) – A quasi-military organization specializing in telekinesis; a complement to the Tararian Guard

Priesthood – The former governing body of the Taran Empire

CAST

Tararian Guard

Kira Elsar – Captain, team leader

Ari Lanmore – Lance corporal, weapons specialist on Kira's team

Kyle Asher – Lance corporal, technical specialist on Kira's team

Nia Boro – Lance corporal, technical specialist on Kira's team

Leon Caletti – Civilian consultant, geneticist/scientist, Kira's significant other

Terence Kaen – Colonel, Kira's chain-of-command

Lucas Sandren – Major, Kira's commanding officer

Deanna Olvera – Major, Orion Station head of security

Doctor Elric – Lead medical doctor for Orion Station base

Allen Lucian – General, leader of Orion Station base

Elusian Alliance *(member world of Taran Empire)*

Elton Joris – President

Ellen Caletti – Press Secretary, former Mysaran spy (Leon's sister)

Nico – Assistant to President Joris

Mysaran Coalition *(independent world)*

Cynthia Hale – Chancellor

MTech *(Research company based on Mysar; branch on Valta)*

Monica Waylon – Director of MTech's lab on Valta (deceased)

Jared Frey – Monica's research assistant at the MTech lab

LOCATIONS

Orion Station – Tararian Guard base

Elvar Trinary – Kira's home system (planets: Mysar, Valta, Elusia)

Tararia – The central planet of the Taran Empire

CHAPTER 1

EYES WEREN'T SUPPOSED to glow orange. Captain Kira Elsar was positive about that fact, and she was especially sure that *her* eyes should be nothing other than hazel.

She backed away from the bathroom mirror. *What the fok happened?*

Kira's mind pored over the events from the last several days—her infiltration of the MTech research facility, her struggle with the mad scientist, Monica, and… the prick on her wrist.

"Oh, fok," she whispered.

Her medical exam had come back clear. Everything had seemed fine until this moment. But Monica must have given her the treatment that she had been working on in her secret lab—an experimental strain of nanites.

But Kira didn't want to be anything other than herself, let alone some freakish alien hybrid Robus with fifteen-centimeter claws, enhanced strength, super speed, and stars knew what else. Well, admittedly, the speed and strength would be perks, but that was beside the point.

Leon! With sudden panic, she remembered her ex-boyfriend turned second chance lover waiting in her bed. Her hopes to rekindle the relationship would most certainly meet a premature end if she slashed his face off.

She slammed the door to the bathroom and locked it.

"Everything okay in there?" Leon called from the next room, having roused to the sound.

"Uh… we might have a problem," Kira replied.

"What is it?"

"Um…." She thought about what to say. *Well, can't exactly hide foking orange glowy eyes.* She swallowed. "So, remember when you thought you saw Monica slip me a shot while we were fighting in the lab?"

"Yeah."

"Well, looks like I was dosed after all."

Running footfalls sounded in the other room. "Kira, what's happening?" His voice was just on the other side of the door.

Kira looked in the mirror. "My eyes are orange."

"Kira! What…?"

"Nothing else seems off, though," she added. "But I saw what those things did in the lab. If I transform completely, I don't know if I'd be myself. I don't want to hurt you."

"Well, a tiny bathroom isn't the best place for you to be right now. We need to get you somewhere where we can run tests and figure out what's going on."

"Leon, you are being entirely too calm and rational right now, considering I just told you I might be infected with alien nanotech!"

"Losing my shite won't help you."

Stars, she wished she could kiss him through the door. *I am never letting this guy go again.* She took a deep breath. "Thank you."

"Now, if I recall, Melissa didn't shift as long as she was calm," Leon continued. "I know you're freaking out right now, but take slow, steady breaths and clear your mind."

Kira did as she was instructed. Her heartrate slowed, and she felt she was in control.

After a minute, she looked in the mirror and saw the orange was fading from her eyes.

"That worked! Fok, why is this happening?" She unlocked the door and slid it open.

Leon was waiting for her on the other side. His brow was furrowed, and his violet eyes searched hers. "Looks normal now."

"I don't want to be a Robus." Kira wrapped her arms around him, and he held her close.

"It's all technology. We can find a way to fix this, or at least to keep you from turning against your will."

"Don't make promises you might not be able to keep." She pulled away. "Let's get me into a holding cell while I'm myself. No telling what might happen next."

"Right." Leon took her hand and squeezed it. "I'm here for you no matter what, okay?"

Kira placed a hand on the side of his face. "Thanks. Nice job talking me down."

"I have a gift." He gave her a quick kiss.

She ran her fingers through his hair, relishing the contact. There was no telling when they might be alone and close together again.

"We should get dressed," she murmured as their lips parted.

They put on their shipsuits in silence. Thoughts of her future flashed through Kira's head. As much as she wanted to think that Leon's advanced training in genetics would help save her from this apparent affliction, she had little hope there would be a treatment for her. To the best of her knowledge, once someone had nanites in their body, it was almost impossible to eradicate the tech. Whatever she was becoming, might be the new normal.

When they were dressed, Leon extended his hand. "I'm with you. It's going to be fine."

She entwined her fingers in his. "I hope so."

They hurried from the lower left arm of the star-shaped Orion Station—the Tararian Guard base Kira called home—to the medical facilities in the center of the structure.

Upon reaching the reception area, Kira released Leon's hand and stepped forward. "I'm submitting myself for placement into quarantine."

The intake nurse's eyes widened. "What for? Have you been exposed to a contagion?"

"No, nothing like that."

"Then why do you suggest quarantine?" the nurse asked.

"Because a few minutes ago I had orange, glowing eyes, and I might turn into an alien monster at any second."

The nurse took a step back. "I'll get the doctor." She ran across the room.

"It's just my foking luck." Kira sighed.

"On the positive side, now we know what Monica gave you, at least," Leon pointed out. "I was worried it might be some sort of sleeper attack thing where we'd forget there was ever a problem, and then ten years from now someone would say just the right words to activate you, and you'd go on a murder spree."

"Still might go on a murder spree with this whole deal." Kira circled her face with her index finger.

"You won't lose touch with yourself." Leon looked her in

the eyes. "We'll get through this, Kira."

She was about to respond when the nurse ran back across the infirmary with the doctor who'd given Kira a medical all-clear not an hour prior.

"What seems to be the problem now?" Doctor Elric asked.

"Well, Doctor, I looked in the mirror and my eyes were glowing orange."

He frowned. "They're not now."

"Yes, I'm aware of that," Kira replied. "I think I was injected with Robus nanites."

The doctor stared at her blankly.

"Did you not read the mission report?" Kira took a calming breath. "You know what, just lock me up and call Colonel Kaen."

"Wh—" the doctor began.

Kira set off across the infirmary toward the isolation chambers she'd seen on her previous visits. "I'll just see myself in."

Leon and the doctor followed her.

"I can't say I've ever had a patient so insistent to be quarantined," Doctor Elric said.

"It's best not to argue with her when she's made up her mind," Leon advised.

"And you are?" Elric asked.

Leon hesitated and looked to Kira. They hadn't placed a title on their relationship status yet.

"Leon Calleti, the Guard's newest civilian consultant—genetics research," Kira replied for him. "And he's with me."

"As in, to be locked up, as well?" the doctor prompted.

Kira sighed. "No, as in a partner—someone with vested interest in my wellbeing. If I'm not myself, I give permission for him to speak on my behalf."

Leon met her gaze, his mouth parted with surprise.

She gave him a smile of affirmation as she reached the quarantine chamber's entrance. The plexiglass box was on par with the facilities Kira had seen in the MTech research labs, and she was confident it would be able to hold her even if she lost control in Robus form.

Doctor Elric made an entry on the keypad next to the chamber, and a transparent door slid open with a hiss.

Kira stepped into the entry tunnel, which ran the depth of the room parallel to the main space. "We'll talk this through with Colonel Kaen."

She pressed the button inside to cycle the chamber. The exterior door closed and an interior panel in the side of the tunnel slid open. Though the setup was equipped with bolts, no security lock protocols were presently engaged.

Kira stepped into the room and walked up to the front window next to the entry tunnel. She placed her hand on the plexiglass.

Leon touched his fingertips to hers on the other side of the barrier. "I'll meet with my new team. We'll figure this out." His voice sounded hollow through the filter of the comm system.

"You need to talk to Jared," Kira told him.

Leon scowled. "I want nothing to do with that piece of shite."

"He helped Monica do whatever was done to me. If it can be undone, he may know how."

He nodded. "All right, I'll make the arrangements to interview him."

"No, not interview," Kira shook her head. "Interrogate. And if he doesn't want to talk, I'll pull the answers straight out his head myself."

"Oh, fok!" Leon jumped back from the glass.

"What?"

"Your eyes…"

Kira turned away and retreated into the room, willing herself to calm. *You're still you. You're in control.*

She placed a hand on her stomach and took slow, steady breaths with her eyes closed. Nothing in the outside universe mattered. She was alive, and she was happy.

The tension released from her body.

When she turned back around to face Leon, he smiled and nodded.

"Back to normal," he confirmed. "I believed you, of course, but seeing it for myself…"

She smirked. "You mean, you don't like the glow of Fury in my eyes?"

"It's, uh, a bit disconcerting."

"You're tellin' me." Kira sighed. "Has the doctor called Kaen?"

"I can go check," Leon offered.

"Please stay. You can talk me down again if I start to turn. I don't think any of us want to find out what would happen if I do."

Leon's face paled, but he stepped up to the window. "You're not like those other people they experimented on. You've been trained, and conditioned—"

"I might have my telepathic abilities, but that's not the same thing. No amount of Guard training could have prepared me for this."

"Regardless, I'd wager that you're at least twice as stubborn as any other soldier. You won't lose yourself as easily as you seem to think."

"Yeah, I'll show them how it's done." Kira forced a smile, but she had her doubts. *I should have known some foking shite like this would happen. Everything was going too perfectly.* She released a long breath and suppressed the negative thoughts. *No, I'll beat this.*

As she returned to a more rational state, Kira spotted Colonel Kaen and Doctor Elric approaching from the direction of the infirmary's entry.

Leon stepped back from the glass, giving a nod of deference to the colonel.

"Kira, what seems to be the trouble?" Kaen asked.

"I believe Monica gave me a dose of the Robus nanites," she replied. "I don't know why it didn't show up in my medical exam."

The colonel seemed surprisingly calm. "You said your eyes have changed? They seem normal now."

"I saw it, sir," Leon interjected. "They seem to change when she's distressed."

Except I wasn't upset when they changed the first time, Kira realized. "*Aroused* might be a better characterization" she said. "And no, I don't mean 'turned on'. I was happy the first time it happened. It could be tied to any strong emotion."

"That's possible," Doctor Elric mused.

Kira frowned. "Unfortunately, suppressing my emotions isn't exactly my strong suit."

"We'll research the nanites and determine if there's a way to reverse the effects. Even if there isn't, you can certainly gain control of the new abilities," Kaen jumped in.

He sounded awfully confident, considering what Kira had just told him.

Kira didn't care for that perspective. "Sir, it's one thing to be born a certain way—or to make a conscious choice to be modified—but I didn't sign up for this." Her skin tingled as anger about what MTech had done to her swelled inside her.

"Huh. Well that *is* fascinating," Kaen said while Doctor Elric's jaw dropped.

"My eyes have changed again, haven't they?" Kira's voice sounded wrong to her ears. In fact, all her senses were off. She suddenly had a more acute awareness of her surroundings—from the breathing of those on the other side of the glass, to the air scrubbers filtering the air within the chamber.

Leon swallowed and took a step back. "It's not just your eyes this time."

Fok me. Kira looked down at her hands, which were now coated in seemingly metallic scales above her normal skin, covering her entire body. Her fingers ended in long, silvery claws, and her exposed hands and arms were now augmented with what looked like bands of muscle beneath the scaly second-skin.

Her shipsuit was nowhere to be seen. Startled, she realized that part of the decking where she'd been standing was also gone.

"What the…?" She sensed a coating in her mouth that had reshaped her teeth to sharp points.

"You're still… you?" Leon questioned.

Kira stepped out of the shallow hole in the deck. "I don't understand."

"Perhaps the nanites needed material to replicate," Doctor Elric mused. "How do you feel?"

"Okay, I guess. Can't say I have murdery impulses. Well, no more than I would after Ari has uploaded a new one of his videos," Kira replied. Her voice still sounded strange.

She turned from the window to see if there was a reflective surface somewhere in the chamber.

At the back, she found a door into a compact washroom. Above the sink there was a mirror, but she didn't recognize the face staring back at her.

The metallic scales extended up her neck and covered most of her face. The appearance of enhanced muscle mass on her arms was present over the rest of her body, most notably her shoulders, chest, and thighs. The orange glow of her eyes was now overshadowed by a scaled plating wrapping from her brow, over the top of her head, and down her back. She still couldn't tell if *she* had transformed or if the nanites had activated some sort of armor around her that was also somehow a part of her. She'd expected to be horrified by the transformation, but there was something striking about it—beautiful in its raw power.

Okay, so I can understand why they'd take a step back. Kira tapped one of her fangs with her claws. *Holy fok, I have fangs and claws!*

Despite her initial declaration that she had no interest in being modified, she did have to admit that it had some appeal. For the entire time she'd been with her team, they had been stronger and faster than her. They'd never admit it to her face, but she knew there were times when they wished they could race ahead and get the mission done in their own way. If she had all their skills, and more, well... that would make her indispensable.

Could this be a good thing? Scared and confused, she willed herself to return to calm—to return to herself. The metallic scales liquified and began flowing back into her.

Kira's nerves ignited as though she were being incinerated. A raspy cry escaped her lips as she collapsed to the ground in writhing agony.

CHAPTER 2

"KIRA!" SHE HEARD someone shout in the distance.

Shouts of protest followed, and then the hiss of a sealed door opening.

Firm hands gripped her wrists, and another set cradled her face and stroked the top of her head.

"Stay with me," Leon murmured.

The pain receded, and Kira's senses dimmed. Slowly, she opened her eyes.

Leon was bent over her, supporting her head in his lap. Doctor Elric and Colonel Kaen each held one of her wrists, which they released when they saw her open eyes.

"What happened?" Kira murmured.

"You transformed and everything seemed fine, then we heard you scream, and I came running in," Leon explained.

"Bomaxed fool," Kaen muttered. "She could have sliced you to ribbons with those claws."

"I couldn't just leave her writhing on the ground!" Leon shot back.

"We need to run some tests," Doctor Elric said as he rose

to his feet. "It's encouraging to see you remained lucid when you first transformed, but this situation is unprecedented."

Kira sat up with Leon's help. "How do we get these things out of me?"

"It's too early to say," the doctor replied. He grabbed a sheet off the bed and handed it to her.

It was then Kira realized that she was completely naked. She wrapped the sheet around herself. "Thanks."

Leon helped her the rest of the way to her feet.

"We need to commence testing before you have another seizure, or whatever that was," Doctor Elric interjected. "I know you won't like this suggestion, but I feel it would be best if we restrain you on the bed. That way, we can work on you without risk of harm to us or yourself."

Kira nodded. "I'll hate it when I'm my normal self, but you got lucky this last time. I saw those claws—those'll do serious damage."

"The bed restraints are strong enough to hold someone even in powered armor, so they should be sufficient," the doctor said. "We'll move you to the next room where there isn't a hole in the deck." He glanced at the damaged tiles.

"I'll lend any assistance I can with testing," Leon offered the doctor while they relocated to the adjacent isolation chamber. "I'm still not up to speed on the nanotech side of things, but I can advise on the biological interactions."

Doctor Elric inclined his head. "I welcome any help. Robus are new to me."

Leon nodded. "To all of us."

"This case is a priority," Colonel Kaen stated.

The doctor bristled. "I give the best possible care to all my patients, sir."

In the new isolation chamber, Kira sat down on the bed,

still holding the sheet around herself.

Elric turned on the display for the analytical array at the head of the bed. "Huh," he said. "It looks like you've gained weight."

The comment caught Kira off-guard. "Maybe my meal portions have been a little larger than normal over the past few days, but is this really the time to talk about dieting?"

He shook his head. "No, as in, you've gained a *lot* of weight—more than twenty kilos since your med eval yesterday. I believe that supports the hypothesis that the nanites converted the available material to replicate. The efficiency of matter transmutation is astounding. Limited heat, no radiation. I've never seen tech like this."

"You mean, the deck and my shipsuit are… inside me now?"

"We won't know more until I can get a proper look at those nanites. I'll grab the sampling kit." Doctor Elric headed for the door.

"I'll get you a new uniform," Kaen told Kira and followed the doctor out.

"Oh, thank you, sir." Kira bit her lower lip. *Shite, if the colonel is running errands for me, I really must be in bad shape.*

Leon took Kira's hands when they were alone. "Are you feeling okay now?"

"Yeah, I think so. This is all so… sudden."

He stroked the side of her face. "Just to be clear, I don't regret coming here to the Guard, even if my girlfriend is now some sort of super-mutant." He grinned.

Kira punched him lightly in the arm.

He laughed. "Were it anyone else, I'd be concerned. I think you'll be just fine. And I'll be with you every step of the way."

"You sure about that? You didn't sign up for this."

"Positive."

Kira squeezed his hand. "I'm glad you're here."

The door hissed as Elric returned, testing kit in hand. "All right, Kira, let's figure out what's happening to you." He held up a comically large syringe and a metal rod Kira really didn't want to get to know on an intimate level.

She gulped. "Yay."

— — —

Colonel Terence Kaen entered the supply room and located a rack of shipsuits. He normally would have ordered support staff to retrieve such an item for him, but he was driven by an impulse to handle the matter himself—to find somewhere private.

"*You care for your subordinates, I can tell,*" a voice said in Kaen's mind.

Kaen froze in the center of the enclosed room. "*The fok...? Who—*"

"*There, there, no reason to be frightened. You and I will be such good friends,*" the voice soothed.

Kaen wanted to run for help, but his limbs wouldn't obey his commands. His heart pounded in his ears.

"*You've been a good host,*" a voice replied in his mind, "*but it's time for me to be in charge. I must make sure Kira matures into who we wish her to be.*"

A memory roused deep within, striking Kaen with a sharp pain.

His pulse quickened as memories flooded back to him. None of it made any sense. He saw himself doing things he'd never dream of doing.

"*What's happening?*" He gripped his head. "*Who are you?*"

"I am one of many. We found Valta long ago, used it as a place to learn and grow. We have since moved, but now the time has come to expand."

This being was alien—a sentient form beyond the Taran sphere. The Bakzen had been one thing, but this… This wasn't how Kaen pictured a first contact scenario for his people.

"I went to Valta for one mission and you hop aboard like I'm some type of transport?" Kaen's breath was ragged. *"Get the fok out!"*

The voice chuckled. *"Oh, no. I've been here for much longer than the recent mission to Valta."*

The jumble of memories began to clear in Kaen's mind.

He had traveled to Mysar—a trip three years prior, he remembered—but these recollections were different. He had met with Chancellor Hale, and she was also not who she appeared to be. She was like him, a puppet being directed by some unseen force.

Kaen saw himself meeting with each of the subjects he'd interviewed during his recent interrogations, to gather information from them and to subvert them through telepathic influence. For years, he'd been manipulating them behind the scenes.

And then there was the recent incident with the MTech lab. First, he'd sent Kira on the op, knowing she was the perfect subject for the final stage of their experimentation. He'd allowed Monica to escape after they'd taken her into custody, standing by while she took out everyone around him and then went back to infect Kira with the nanites. He and Monica were working together—until she was killed. She had been a willing participant, following directions issued by their masters. But the mission didn't end with her death.

Kaen and Hale were there to finish the job.

"Do you understand now?" the voice asked.

It was becoming clear, yes, but he was horrified by the implications. Maybe this wasn't a first contact at all. *"You've been with me since my trip to Mysar, but I don't understand how this is possible."*

If Kaen had had any control over his body, he'd try to carve the being out of him on the spot. Instead, he could only stand there motionless in the supply closet, desperately trying to process the harm that had been caused by his actions.

"Don't struggle now. You wouldn't want to harm us," the voice cautioned.

He was still unable to move. *"Are you in my head?"*

"Yes, in a sense," the voice affirmed. *"But I am one with you."*

"Leave!" Kaen shouted in his mind. *"I'll slice you out myself."*

"I rather like it here. You are already a man of influence, though I could help you gain even more. You've already been so useful with directing our other tools."

"What are you after?" Kaen asked the voice.

"We have much to discuss," the voice replied. *"It's time we get to know one another."*

Kaen listened as the alien being filled the gaps in Kaen's memory about everything he had done over the past three years. He wanted nothing more than to turn himself in, but he was now a passenger in his own body.

Transforming Kira into a Robus was all according to plan. Whose plan that was, exactly, remained a mystery to him. All he knew for certain was that the entity inside him wasn't working alone. Beyond the Mysaran Chancellor, Hale—who was also being controlled by a similar entity—there were a number of willing collaborators as well as others who had been subverted. He didn't yet understand how the alien beings' abilities worked, or the extent of their power, but he knew they meant harm.

Yet, Kaen's only option for the time being was to go along for the ride. He remembered now what it had been like when the mysterious being first possessed him—that if he tried to resist too much, his possessor would push Kaen's consciousness further to the back of his mind where he couldn't even see what was happening. He'd learned that as long as he remained quiet and unobtrusive, he could at least remain apprised of the unfolding situation. He decided that was the strategy he needed to adopt now, waiting for opportunities to inject little bits of influence here and there; even the smallest act might make a difference at the right moment.

The alien being had understood the importance of keeping up appearances. Acts like getting Kira a new shipsuit to accommodate her condition demonstrated a level of caring compassion that the being wouldn't have voluntarily elected to do, but Kaen's recommendation still held weight. The being listened, and that gave Kaen hope.

While Kira struggled with her transformation, Kaen would be fighting his own internal battle. This creature of thought was fascinated by Kira, giving Kaen the chance to help her. Maybe, one day, she'd be able to help him, in turn.

"What's been set in motion cannot be stopped." The alien taunted him. *"At least you will be on the winning side."*

Kaen allowed the alien its feeling of superiority. His chance would come. *"How do I address you, now that you are no longer a silent companion?"*

"You may call me Nox," the voice replied.

Kaen had heard that name before. He thought back to the

first interrogation he'd conducted for the recent investigation. *"That was Captain Ellis' supposed contact, wasn't it?"*

"Yes, a role you played so well."

Kaen shuddered as he thought back to the interrogations over the past several days—the people he'd subverted without even knowing what he'd done, or how he'd done it. And now they'd suffer because of his actions.

"You're a tool, just like them," Nox said with a mental jab.

Kaen ignored the entity's statement.

"We shouldn't keep Kira waiting." Nox directed Kaen back to the infirmary.

When he arrived, he saw Doctor Elric was completing his examination of Kira, and Leon had a blood sample in hand.

Kira smiled when she saw Kaen. "I was surprised when you offered to get me a new suit yourself, sir. Recent moments have made me especially grateful for someone who offers help in a way that doesn't involve drawing blood or sticking something in me."

A playful look passed between Kira and Leon, and she smirked. "Well, maybe it's not *all* bad," she added quietly.

"If you want a treatment for this condition, then this is a necessary part of the process," Elric said, having missed the innuendo.

Kaen could feel Nox's annoyance with the banter.

"This shipsuit is a little larger size and should accommodate a transformation." Kaen-Nox handed the garment to Kira.

"Thank you, Colonel." Kira paused. "I know I'm under quarantine, but I'd like permission to speak with Major Sandren."

Kaen-Nox tensed. "Why?"

"I just want to keep him in the loop, sir. My team will be

wondering where I am."

"Yes, of course." Kaen-Nox nodded.

"Thank you, sir."

"I should get going on this analysis," Leon said in the ensuing silence.

"As should I. Try to stay calm and relaxed," Elric advised.

Kira eyed the restraints next to the bed. "Yeah, I'll try." She ran her hands over the shipsuit. "I need to get dressed first."

"I'll secure you after you change," Kaen-Nox told her. "Please proceed with your tests," he addressed Leon and the doctor.

"Yes, sir." Elric nodded and left.

"I'll come back to check on you soon." Leon squeezed Kira's hand.

"See you then." She rose from the bed and headed for the washroom.

Kaen-Nox waited for her with his hands clasped behind his back.

"You and your frail forms. So many precautions needed to keep you safe," Nox commented.

"At least we have our own bodies."

"But isn't it more evolved to be able to be anywhere or in anything?"

Kaen didn't have a good response to that. Maybe the being inside him was more advanced, but that didn't give it the right to take over the body of another sentient individual.

Kira emerged from the washroom wearing the new shipsuit, carrying the ripped old one. "Well, sir, the outer layer is a little bigger than regulation specs," she tugged on the loose fabric at her stomach, "but it'll get the job done."

"We must always be prepared."

"Yes, sir." She paused. "Sir, may I speak freely?"

"Granted." Nox made the metal equivalent of an eyeroll.

"You've seen people go through war and come out the other side as someone different," Kira continued. "How do you define your identity when you change like that, needing to become a different person acting in a different role?"

"If only she knew how apt of a question that was for us," Nox commented.

"I don't think of it as going from one person to another, but rather as two facets of the same person," Kaen recited at Nox's direction. "I know you're wrestling with some significant physical changes that most people would never experience, but you're still you. Is it really so different when you transform from soldier into lover? Or captain into daughter? Those parts of us exist at all times, but we filter our surroundings based on the context of whatever role we're playing in a given moment."

Kira nodded. "Hmm, I hadn't thought about it that way."

Kaen had to admit, Nox answered better than what he would have said himself.

Nox continued feeding Kaen words to speak, "I can't imagine what it would be like to become something else after so many years in one form—"

"Yeah, right," Kaen quipped to Nox in his mind.

"—but I do appreciate what it's like to have your responsibilities change. I worked my way up in my career just like everyone else, and I've gone from being one soldier among many to being part of a small group of senior officers. With each advancement came a new sense of identity."

Kaen-Nox looked Kira in her eyes. "You, Kira, are now advancing, as well. You have been gifted for your whole life, and you've used those gifts to help the Guard accomplish what few others could have done. Now, you'll have even more skills to bring to bear. I am confident you will master these new attributes and be truly one of a kind."

Kira shifted on the bed. "I appreciate that, sir, but I don't know if I'd keep these abilities, if given the choice. I know there are benefits, but there are also risks."

"You must keep them."

Kira frowned and inched back on the bed. "May I ask why, sir?"

Kaen-Nox softened and smiled, realizing the statement had been too forceful. "Rather, you should take some time to evaluate your new skills before you decide to permanently dismiss them, assuming the nanites can be removed. It's only been, what, half an hour? That's not enough time to consider the pros and cons of the situation."

"I guess it's not."

"Get some rest, Captain. Leon and Doctor Elric will be able to tell you more about your options soon."

"Right." Kira swung her legs up onto the bed and reclined, placing her hands at her sides. "I hope they can tell me how to stop random transformations more definitively than just *stay calm.*"

"You'll gain control. I have no doubts." Kaen-Nox cinched the bed's restraint cuffs around her wrists.

"I thought you'd be more concerned about me being a potential security risk."

"You're plenty secure now."

"But what about my telepathic abilities? How might that interact with the Robus nanotech?" Kira asked.

Kaen-Nox smiled. "We'll wait and see."

— — —

Kira watched Colonel Kaen leave the room. Something

about him seemed different from the man she'd known before the mission to Valta. She couldn't place what exactly, but it seemed unlikely the security-conscious officer she'd known would be content to leave her with only a couple of restraints in the middle of a Guard base. After all, she was carrying unknown nanotech inside her, and that could do *anything*.

Kira expected him to have flipped his shite when he learned about her condition but, instead, he seemed calm. But not just calm, almost... pleased.

That's not possible, Kira dismissed with a shake of her head. *Right?*

She couldn't think of a reason that might explain his behavior. More likely, he was acting normally and it was *her* perception that was off.

She squirmed around on her bed to get comfortable, but there was no way she was going to feel at ease while strapped down. Moreover, there were too many uncertain thoughts running through her head.

I trust Leon to figure out what's going on with me, but maybe Kaen is right. Maybe this is something for me to embrace rather than run from. Kira hated the idea of such a fundamental life change being thrust upon her with no warning, but it wasn't like she'd planned on having telepathic abilities, either. She was shocked, and then she adapted.

With special skills came the likelihood she would be used—just like the people on her home of Valta wanted her to become a Reader, and just like the Guard used her now for their covert investigations.

She was a willing participant in the latter, but how many new 'special assignments' would she get if she were a telepath *and* a super-soldier?

The team dynamic would change, that was for sure. But

her team was her family. She wanted to stay with them and to work together—it's what made her work fulfilling. Losing that companionship was the last thing she wanted to change.

Her thoughts were interrupted by a knock on the plexiglass window looking out into the hall. She looked over to see Doctor Elric holding up a handwritten sign.

Why the fok would he be writing something out on a dry erase board rather than typing it? In true doctor fashion, his handwriting was almost indecipherable. She squinted at the script to make it out: 'Kaen isn't who he seems.'

Kira's heart dropped. She shook her head with confusion.

Elric erased the message on the whiteboard and wrote another: 'Play along.'

Before she could question him, the doctor departed.

What in the stars was that about? Kira released a long sigh and nestled into her pillow. If the colonel was indeed not who he seemed, then things would be getting very uncomfortable, fast. He was a senior officer, and not a lot of people in the Guard would have the authority to detain him on suspicions alone. The doctor had better have some sort of evidence to support the odd behavior of handwritten notes.

Kira groaned. *And the day had gotten off to such a good start.*

CHAPTER 3

LEON'S LAB SETUP in Orion Station's science wing was a far cry from his previous arrangement at MTech, but he hadn't exactly had time to do any customizing yet. Colonel Kaen had indicated that Leon would have a budget to purchase anything he might need to continue MTech's nanotech and genetics research in a more civilized and ethical fashion, but having a budget meant little without also having the time to acquire those materials.

He looked over the equipment at his disposal and frowned. *This won't get the job done.*

The lab had also come with two assistants, who'd been pulled off related research assignments with medical applications. They watched Leon from their chairs on the other side of the room.

"Something wrong?" Jack asked.

"You don't have a sequencer," Leon replied. "How am I supposed to run any sort of analysis without a sequencer?"

"Well, we sorta do," Tess countered. "It's just not the type you're used to." She rose from her chair and crossed the seven-meter-wide space to a console along the wall near Leon. She opened a door in the console and produced a fifty-centimeter-square box.

"And that is…?" Leon prompted.

"The old-fashioned way of doing things," Tess replied. "Breaks everything down and tells you how it ticks."

"Organic analysis? I didn't realize the Taran Empire still did things this way."

"Well, most labs don't," Jack responded, "but this kind of research hasn't historically been a part of the Guard. This equipment is old."

Leon groaned. "Using this, we'll have to translate the components to their digital representations to create an expression model."

"Unless you know of another sequencer, then this is what we have to work with," Tess replied with a shrug.

"I know exactly where we can get one, but I don't know if they'll allow it." Leon crossed his arms.

"Where?" questioned Jack.

"The MTech lab on Valta."

Tess screwed up her face. "Wasn't that place condemned after your op?"

"It wasn't *my* op, it—" He shook his head. "Never mind. Yes, it was condemned, but that was to keep the locals out. Lots of debris and equipment where a person could get hurt. But if you know your way around, there's lots of good tech to be obtained."

Jack frowned. "That's private MTech property."

"Yes, which is why I said the Guard might not allow it."

Tess pursed her lips. "Even with transit time to the Elvar Trinary, we'd still save time versus an organic analysis."

"My thoughts, too," Leon agreed. "*If* I can get permission to go."

"Give it a shot," Jack said. "We'll get going on the organic sampling in case you can't swing it."

"Maybe I can find us some other goodies, too." Leon smiled. "By the way, thanks for jumping in to help with this."

Jack shrugged. "The chance to study genuine alien tech? That's not something any sane scientist would pass up."

Leon's eyes narrowed the slightest measure. "Remember, this tech is connected to a person, and I happen to care about her very much. Her name is Kira, and she's not just a subject."

Tess grinned. "Ooo, I see what kind of assignment this is! We're not just here for science, but we have to save the love of our boss' life."

Jack chuckled. "That's a nice little bit of motivation."

Leon sighed. "She's not…" No, he wouldn't kid himself—not after the years he'd tried to forget Kira and pretend that his career was enough to fulfill him. Some bonds were too strong and ran too deep. They'd been lucky to meet each other young, but it was before they knew what it meant to be a partner to someone, and they'd tossed it away. Now, they were back together, and he wouldn't let her go again. He saw in Kira's eyes, even when they were crazy Robus orange, that she felt the same way. Leon had to do everything he could to either make Kira's new condition bearable for her or find a way to reverse it.

He looked to his team members. "Yes, she means a lot to me. More than science, I'm here as someone who wants her to have the best future she can. I hope you'll help me give her that."

Tess nodded. "Stars, I'd have done it for just the science. But I'm a sucker for a love story."

"As long as I get an equipment upgrade at the end of this, I'm game for whatever," Jack said.

Leon smiled with satisfaction. "Then I have an MTech lab to raid."

— — —

The voice in Kaen's head had been quiet since the chat with Kira, following the revelation in the supply closest when everything had become so clear. Now knowing his part in the recent Guard security breach, Kaen reevaluated everything he thought he'd learned during the investigation. He felt a twang of remorse for the fates the other Guard members would suffer as a result of his actions.

But Nox had a vision, and Kaen was powerless to deviate from that plan. It had all been explained to Kaen with such conviction that he almost believed it was the best course. Almost. Kaen was determined to resist, despite being relegated to backstage in his own body and mind.

From deep within himself, he sensed his body returning to his office—a place that was as much his home as any residence he'd ever had as a child. He looked around the place with new eyes, absorbing the details for what was now an unrestricted control room from which to orchestrate plans with civilization-scale impacts.

"It's so impersonal," Nox commented, looking over the unadorned desktop and walls. *"Then again, you* are *a loner."*

"You already know everything that's in my mind, yet you still comment and ask questions," Kaen replied.

"Come now, Terence. What did I say before? We are to be the best of friends."

"Then tell me," Kaen demanded, *"how many others have I subverted?"*

Nox gave him a mental tsk. *"I can't give away all my secrets, can I?"*

"So, you probably won't tell me how many others there are like you."

"*There are... enough.*"

"*What are you after?*" Kaen asked.

"*We are hungry.*"

"*For what?*"

"*In time, it will become clear,*" was Nox's only response.

Kaen-Nox turned his attention to catching up on communications that had stacked up while he was gone. He scanned through the list of electronic messages, mostly copies of memos to keep him in the loop rather than anything requiring direct action.

One particular message, though, caught his eye. It was from the alias account he'd used for his written correspondence with the Elusian president: >>Chancellor Hale may not be herself. Possible connection to the subversions within the Guard. Investigate immediately.<<

"*Oh, can't let anyone else see rumors like that!*" Nox said.

"*How long has the chancellor been subverted?*" Kaen tried to ask, but the presence controlling him suppressed the thought.

"*Don't worry yourself. You'll be in good company soon.*"

Kaen watched his hand select the message, send a generic acknowledgment, and then delete the original.

"*See? It's nothing at all,*" Nox said. "*Now, what else do we have?*"

The next message that caught Kaen-Nox's eye was a follow-up communication regarding the sentencing for the three individuals who had violated security. It grated on Kaen's conscience that he had been the one to subvert them and that they were now being punished because of it.

The lieutenant and captain both had motivations Kaen-Nox had been able to exploit through subtle telepathic prodding, and some mysterious helpers behind the scenes made sure those promises related to outside had been delivered. With Alan, though, Kaen-Nox had simply implanted a command for the unlucky communication tech to do his bidding and then to forget anything had been done. The part of Kaen that was still himself hated the abuse, but he was overpowered by Nox's pleasure.

All the other messages could wait for another time. There was a more pressing matter.

Nox's presence filled Kaen's mind. *"You must guide Kira in her new abilities. Prepare her for us."*

— — —

Major Lucas Sandren had lost good soldiers over the years, but having one transformed into a new type of being was a novel experience. He scowled as Colonel Kaen relayed the news about Kira's uncertain condition to him in his office.

The colonel was surprisingly calm about the whole thing, so maybe it wasn't as big of a deal as it sounded. But Sandren knew Kira, and he was certain that no matter how calm she might appear on the outside, she'd be filled with uncertainty and concern over what this change meant for her.

"I'd like to talk with Kira," Sandren requested when Kaen finished his explanation.

"She already asked to speak with you," Kaen assented. "I think she wanted you to fill in her team."

"Oh, right. Not looking forward to that conversation."

"She's alive and doesn't appear to be in any immediate danger. I look at this as an opportunity," Kaen stated.

Sandren was taken aback. "Sir, our people aren't commodities. I suspect Kira didn't want this. We have to do what's best for her."

"Oh, of course. I didn't mean to imply otherwise."

"Well, I'll check in on Kira and see how she's doing," Sandren stated. "But, sir, I do recognize that her telepathy is a unique asset to this organization and that having additional augmentations would make her that much more valuable."

"Yes, her care is our top priority." Without another word, Kaen departed.

Sandren slumped in his desk chair and took a moment to gather his thoughts before heading to the infirmary.

When he arrived in the medical center, Sandren headed for the quarantine rooms in the back, where he had been informed Kira was being held. His chest constricted when he saw her strapped to the medical bed like a criminal. "Kira..." He stepped up to the window.

"Hey, Major. I don't think I'm about to rip your face off if you want to come in to talk," she greeted.

Sandren entered through the containment tunnel and approached her bed. "Why did they strap you down like this?"

"I changed earlier and then blacked out in some sort of seizure. This is as much for me as it is to make sure I don't hurt anyone." She stared down at her feet. "I like to think I'll be able to hold onto myself, but I'm not sure I can."

"We're all here to help you," Sandren tried to assure her, but he really had no idea what he could do aside from offer moral support.

"I wanted to talk about my team," Kira said. "It's important."

"Of course, I'm listening."

"It's *really* important," she emphasized, looking him in the eyes.

Sandren caught on and repositioned so she could look at him straight-on. A moment later, he felt a presence in his mind.

"Doctor Elric came by a few minutes ago. He held up a handwritten sign that said 'Kaen isn't who he seems. Play along.' "

"I don't understand," Sandren replied.

"Have you noticed anything odd about his behavior?"

"Come to think of it, he did seem rather unconcerned with what's happened to you. I'd dismissed it as being his usual detached manner."

Kira swallowed. *"That's what I thought, too. But he told me to embrace this. Who says that to someone who's been infected with an unknown thing?"*

"No Guard officer I know," Sandren told her. *"I'll keep an eye on him."*

"I really appreciate you coming to see me," Kira said aloud. "So, my team... unless they've decided to be heartless asses, they'll be worried about me. Will you let them know I'm okay?"

"Of course, I'll relay a message. I might be able to get them added to the visitor list since you're not *actually* under quarantine."

Kira's gaze passed over her restraints. "I'd rather they not see me like this."

Sandren nodded. "I understand. I'll let them know you—"

"Major Sandren, sorry to interrupt."

Sandren turned around to see Leon standing on the other side of the plexiglass. "I heard you talking about Kira's team. I have a proposition."

"And what is that?" Sandren asked, stepping away from Kira's bed toward the window.

"I don't like where this is going," Kira interjected from the bed. "Not sure I want those social circles to blend."

"If you want out of those restraints faster, then you might want to hold that thought," Leon replied with a wan smile. "Major, I'd like to take Kira's team back to the MTech lab on

Valta to extract some equipment."

"That's not ours to take," Sandren protested.

"It's specialized and can't be purchased from any old supplier," Leon continued. "It'd have to be custom commissioned, and that would take weeks. Without it, we're looking at three days for each test we run here, and we're not going to get what we need the first time. Those tests can be performed in half an hour with the equipment I want to retrieve."

Sandren considered the proposition. "Come to think of it, our official investigation requires a deeper dive into MTech's research practices. I believe we need to send in a team to procure additional evidence from the facility for examination and testing here at Orion Station."

Leon smiled. "I'd like to volunteer myself for that assignment."

"Very well. Approved," Sandren said. "And yes, Kira's team would make for excellent support on the mission since they are already familiar with the facility."

"Thank you, sir. I'll leave as soon as possible."

"I don't like the idea of you going back there," objected Kira.

"It'll be quick. Just grab the equipment and go," Leon told her.

"That's the plan, right. But what about MTech? You think they'll really just let us condemn the lab and not come for their equipment? It's only been a few days since our raid. They might show up around the same time you do."

"Which is why he'll have a team of elite Guard soldiers accompanying him," Sandren countered. "Like I said, this will all be aboveboard as part of the Guard's official investigation. They won't have grounds to bar entry into the facility."

Kira frowned. "It's not getting *in* I'm worried about, sir. It's getting back out."

"I said I'd do anything to help you, Kira, and this is what I have to do," Leon told her.

Sandren looked Kira in the eyes. *"If we want to run detailed analyses to find out what's going on inside you—or Kaen—then this is what we need."*

She sighed. *"You're right. This isn't just about me."*

"Agreed?" Sandren asked aloud.

"All right," Kira conceded. "I appreciate everyone being so willing to jump in to help me."

"We always take care of our own." Sandren stepped toward the door. "I'll keep you apprised."

Kira tugged on her restraints. "You know where to find me."

— — —

"I don't expect them to answer to me," Leon said to Sandren as they walked toward the quarters for Kira's team. "I know I'm an outsider."

"Kira trusts you, so they'll trust you by extension," the major replied.

"As long as they can help move around heavy equipment and handle the shooting if MTech gets nasty, we'll be just fine."

"They have been known to move around some heavy things now and then," Sandren said with a nod. "And they'll work even harder knowing it's for Kira."

The two men reached the door to the shared housing for the three members of Kira's team. While Kira roomed with them when they were on ops and traveling in the *Raven*, she had her own quarters at the Guard base since she was their senior. The three soldiers shared a cabin and were happy to remain together, from what Kira had relayed to Leon.

Sandren knocked on the door

Ari answered. "Major, is everything okay? We were surprised to get your message about a meeting."

"We have some things to discuss. May we come in?" Sandren requested.

Ari sized Leon up, stepping aside.

Leon smiled at Ari and the other soldiers as he entered. He could sense their gazes on him, feeling out his intentions. Regardless of what Sandren had said about their trust for Kira extending to him, Leon was certain he'd have to *earn* their trust, and he intended to do just that.

The cabin was simply appointed, with two beds parallel against the right wall and one across the back, supplemented by a table and four chairs in the front left corner of the room. A door at the midpoint of the left wall presumably led to a washroom.

"We're here about Kira," Sandren began.

"Is she okay?" Ari sat down on the bed closest to the door, and Kyle came to join him.

Nia took a seat at the table with Sandren and Leon. "Why isn't she here with you?"

Leon swallowed. "She's being held in isolation at the moment."

The soldiers' faces paled.

"Sir, what's going on?" Kyle asked Sandren.

"We believe that the MTech scientist, Monica, injected Kira with the Robus nanite strain," he replied.

"No, that's not..." Nia shook her head.

"She's not like the others at the lab," Leon hastily explained. "She fully transformed once and seemed to retain her sense of self."

"So she's, what, the Stage Four subject?" Ari asked. "This is foked up."

"I know it is," Sandren stated. "However, that's the situation we're facing. We'll get what information we can from Monica's assistant, Jared, but Leon also needs some equipment from the MTech lab to run tests on Kira's modifications. It just so happens we, uh, need that very same equipment to further our investigation into MTech—which Leon will oversee."

The soldiers nodded their understanding.

"And we're going in with Leon to get it?" Nia guessed.

"If you'll join me," Leon confirmed. "I'm not as tough as Kira, but I'll do my best to keep up with you. We'll get in and out as quickly as possible."

Ari crossed his muscular arms. "I'm guessing the urgency means you think MTech might come looking to reclaim what was seized."

Leon nodded. "We still have no idea where the orders came from in the organization. Monica may have been acting on her own, or there are others in MTech who'll want to continue the same research."

"And it could extend to the Mysaran government," Kyle pointed out.

"Exactly. Or even beyond." Sandren spread his hands on the table. "This stays between us, but it's possible that Monica didn't subdue you on her own."

Nia scowled. "But who? We were surrounded by Guard soldiers and—"

Sandren held up his finger to silence her. "This stays between us. I'll watch over Kira while you're gone."

The soldiers inclined their heads.

"When can we leave, sir?" Leon asked.

"I'll have the *Raven* prepped for you," Sandren replied. "You can be underway in an hour."

CHAPTER 4

AFTER AN HOUR of being tied down, Kira was already regretting her agreement to be bound. She felt like herself, as much as she knew that could change with a second's notice. But for now, being in complete control of her faculties, it was annoying to be treated like a vicious monster.

To make matters worse, she was alone. When she'd suggested being tethered, Leon had at least been there for company. Now, there was only the background hum of mechanical equipment and an infernal beep coming from an unknown piece of equipment.

"Hello?" Kira called out. *What I wouldn't give to get a viewscreen in here...*

Thirty seconds later, a nurse appeared at the window. "Is everything okay?" she asked.

"I'm going to go stir-crazy. Can I get a book, or a tablet, or something?"

"Sure, we have some tablets for patients. I'll be right back." The nurse disappeared from view.

Not sure how I'll use the thing with these bomaxed cuffs on,

Kira realized. She sighed. The years of being out in the field had made her so impatient with sitting still—not to mention that Leon was off having an adventure without her.

She chuckled, realizing the error in her thinking. There was no way Leon was going to have a good time—not with her team. In fact, he was probably as pinned down as her, even if it wasn't with physical restraints.

Kira made a cluck of pity on Leon's behalf as she thought about what must be going on. *I hope he's up for a workout with those guys.*

The nurse returned with a tablet after a minute. "Now, how are we going to make this work?" she mused, assessing Kira's tethers.

"Maybe you could prop it up on my lap, and then find a separate mouse I could use for navigation?" Kira suggested.

"Good idea." The nurse got to work arranging a pillow to cradle the tablet. "Don't worry, dear. We'll take good care of you until this is resolved."

— — —

Leon dropped his travel bag on the bunk Kira typically used while traveling on the *Raven*.

The three other members of the team were settling into their own bunks, watching him stow the minimal items he'd brought with him. *Kira wasn't exaggerating about how tightknit they are.*

He finished and sat down on his bunk. "Thanks for not objecting to me coming with you on this mission," he said to them with what he hoped was a warm smile.

"You know the equipment we need to get. It's in the best interest of the mission to have you along," Nia said.

"We're doing this for Kira," Kyle responded without looking up from his own activities.

Leon nodded. "I wouldn't expect otherwise." He paused. "I know it's probably strange for you to think of her being in a relationship with anyone."

"She was gone for less than a week and came home with a guy. Yeah, it's a little weird." Nia hopped down from the bunk above Leon's bed to access her locker. "How well could she possibly know you?"

Leon's brow furrowed. "Wait, she didn't tell you about our history? I thought you knew."

"She said you were a friend and went back a long way. What else is there to know?" Ari asked.

"Uh…" Leon let out an uncomfortable laugh. "We dated for four years, when we were teenagers. I thought we were going to get married when we were finished with school, but she ran off to join the Guard instead."

The three soldiers' mouths dropped open.

Nia grabbed a sleep mask and earplugs out of her locker. "So, this was a reconnection, not a new thing."

"Yeah, you could say that." Leon nodded.

"Huh." Nia climbed back up on her bunk.

Leon looked around the room. "Are we good?"

The soldiers shrugged.

"Yeah, you treat Kira right and we'll have your back," Kyle said. "But do anything to hurt her, and you answer to us."

"Gotcha." Leon rose from the bed. "Well, I'm going to get myself acquainted with the ship. I'll see you later."

He departed the cabin and sealed the door behind him. When he was alone in the hall, he released a long breath. *Dealing with her parents is nothing compared to these three. Thank the stars she doesn't have brothers, too!*

Leon wandered down the metal corridor of the residential section in the compact vessel. There were only four cabins, making for cozy living arrangements compared to the spacious environment he was used to on Valta. If it weren't for his time in dormitories while he was in school on Mysar, he doubted he'd have lasted a day on the ship.

The residential hall opened on one side into a small galley. The room was empty while the flight crew prepped the spaceship for departure, so Leon took the opportunity to scope out the rations he'd be consuming for the next few days.

Cabinets along the wall adjoining the hallway were filled with dry goods, and a refrigerator contained meat, vegetables, and an assortment of beverages—neatly organized even to Leon's obsessive standards. All things considered, it was a far better selection than he would have expected. Valta's ecological abundance may have spoiled him, but it was looking like he certainly wouldn't go hungry with the Guard.

A stovetop, oven, and tables with seating for sixteen completed the galley. Leon grabbed a handful of mixed nuts from a container in one of the dried goods cabinets and sat down at the table to eat his snack, oriented so he could look out the bank of viewports on the back wall.

As he was brushing the excess salt from his hands, a man's voice came over the central comm system. "Jumping in one minute."

Leon rose from his seat to get a better view out the viewport, hoping to peek at the navigation beacon before the ship transitioned into subspace. He could just make out the illuminated buoy anchored in a fixed spatial position to serve as a reference point for ships traveling through subspace. It didn't look like much more than a pear-shaped probe the size of a shuttle, but he knew that the tech it housed was what had enabled the Taran Empire to expand. *Crossing between distant star systems in hours… It's still difficult to believe.*

The deck vibrated as the jump drive charged. A haze of shifting blue-green light—a spatial distortion—formed around the ship. The light intensified as the ship slipped into subspace. Time elongated for a moment as they made the transition, and then the starscape was replaced by a sea of ethereal light.

Navigation beacons were positioned at most worlds—sometimes multiple—but the Elvar Trinary had done its best to remain separated from the Taran Empire. There was only a single navigation beacon nearby, located at an intermediary point between four systems, one of which was the Elvar Trinary of Leon's birth. Two of the other systems were uninhabited and used for resource mining, but the third had a permanent ban on entry. Leon wasn't sure why, but he'd been taught from a young age to avoid Gaelon.

The subspace jump to that exit beacon would take a little over two hours, and it would then take the better part of a day to reach their destination at sub-light speeds.

As mesmerizing as the lights in subspace were, Leon decided a better use of his time would be to finish his self-guided tour of the ship. He left the galley and continued down the corridor, which terminated in a ladder, extending up and down. A sign pointing upward indicated the bridge, although he imagined the captain and pilot wouldn't like an uninvited visitor. So, he went down.

Leon got off at the first landing, which looked to be a combination of social space and administrative offices. Workout equipment dotted the room, along with a game table, couch, and an expansive viewscreen on the wall.

Two men were seated on the couch, watching a video.

"Hey," Leon greeted. "I don't think we've met."

"Hi," one of the men replied with surprise. "And you are…?"

"Leon Calleti. I used to work at the MTech lab we're going to investigate."

"Ah, okay, right. You're the one Captain Elsar was partnered with on the last op," the second said.

"Yeah. We grew up together on Valta." Leon moseyed over. "How do you know her?"

"Gil, mechanic," the first man said, pointing to himself with his thumb, then the other man, "and Sven, support systems engineer. Basically, we have nothing to do as long as everything is going right."

Leon nodded. "Sounds like a good gig."

"Except when it's not." Gil shrugged.

"How do you pass the time?" Leon asked. "I've spent my whole life on planets. Being cooped up on a starship is strange to me."

"Well, there's the gym, and the video library, games… But honestly, you want to pick up a hobby. Sven over here has written three novels."

Sven dismissed the statement with a flip of his wrist. "*Novel* is too fancy a term. They were space adventure stories about the team on this ship, as told from the boring perspective of a support systems engineer."

Leon smiled. "Sounds like a prime opportunity to make yourself the hero."

"No one would read about me." He crossed his arms and nestled deeper into the couch. "Not saying I didn't do that, though."

"I'm sure I'll figure out something to do." Leon looked back toward the ladder, debating whether or not to check out the level below to see what else there might be.

"You can join us here, if you like. We were just about to play Fastara with the team before we eat," Gil offered.

"I can't say I've played much."

Sven got a devious glint in his eyes. "That's not a problem."

Unfortunately for Sven, Gil, and the members of Kira's team, Leon's assertion that he was unfamiliar with Fastara was a ruse. Many a night in grad school had been spent competing for prize money to fund a night off-campus, and he'd honed some skills. No need for him to elaborate on his past experience, though. They'd find out soon enough.

— — —

The winter sunlight shining over the Elusian capital was all the sweeter knowing that the Elusian Alliance was now once again a member of the grand Taran Empire. President Elton Joris smiled with satisfaction as he surveyed the city. *We have a bright future ahead of us.*

A knock sounded on his office door.

"Come in."

The door cracked open, and Ellen Calleti poked her head in. "Hello, Mr. President. Do you have a moment?"

"Certainly. Come in, Ellen." Joris gestured to the visitor chair across from his desk and took a seat in his own. "Is this about the integration guidebook?"

"No, but that's coming along well," Ellen replied.

When the Elusian Alliance had signed the reunification agreement with the Taran Empire, new opportunities opened for the Elusian people. President Joris had asked Ellen to draft a summary of those new benefits for citizens to use as a guide. The further they got into the project, the more details they uncovered that Joris knew needed to be documented. Despite the administrative burden, he was excited about the opportunities that would be available to his people in coming generations.

Ellen sat down in the visitor chair and folded her hands over her tablet on her lap. "Actually, sir, I'm here about Chancellor Hale."

"Oh, yes." Joris looked down and sighed. "I reached out to the Guard. My contact said he'd look into it."

Joris had been around politicians long enough to know when a person was dodging a request, and he imagined those same tells extended to members of the military. Given the information Joris had imparted about the Mysaran chancellor potentially being subverted, he would have expected immediate and decisive action. A casual 'look into it' statement didn't come across that way in the slightest.

Ellen frowned, clearly thinking the same thing. "Is there anyone else we can go to?"

"I'm hesitant to take too many backchannels. We're in enough of a political wedge as it is after signing the reunification agreement without representative sign-off."

"But this is a serious threat, sir. If Hale is compromised…"

Joris nodded. "I agree. But it's possible the Guard is taking a more covert approach. I don't want to step on toes."

"Would you like me to do the toe-stepping for you?" Ellen offered.

"What do you have in mind?"

"Well, my brother went to work with the Guard after the MTech lab on Valta was shut down. I could see if he can find out whether an investigation is underway."

Joris smiled. "That's a handy connection to have. But hold off. I'll try a more direct strategy first."

"I'll be standing by." Ellen rose.

"Thank you, Ellen. I'm glad to have you on my side."

She inclined her head. "I'm sorry there was ever a time I wasn't."

Ellen departed, leaving Joris alone with his thoughts.

He leaned back in his chair and steepled his fingers. *Why would the Guard defer an investigation into Hale?* The most obvious explanation was that they already knew something and didn't want to share. If that were the case, he—and Elusia—might not be as safe as he thought.

CHAPTER 5

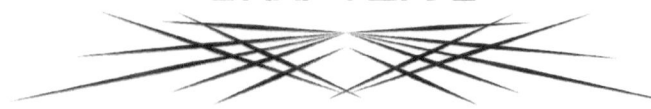

KIRA THUMBED THROUGH the entertainment selection on her tablet. Despite having an entire galaxy's worth of content at her disposal, she still couldn't find anything to watch.

With a heavy sigh, she turned off the tablet with a click of the remote mouse they'd rigged up for her. *Bedtime, I guess. Not that I'm tired after all those naps.* Leon needed to hurry up and get that equipment he needed or else there might not be anything of Kira's mind left to save.

She chuckled to herself. *Wow, I'm a terrible patient.*

Kira was willing to give herself some leeway, though, considering that Doctor Elric's tests had all come back inconclusive. She wouldn't know the extent of her modifications until Leon had a chance to complete his analysis of the new nanites. That could take days.

The thought of waiting in limbo for that long upset Kira all over again, so she closed her eyes with the hope that sleep would pass the time.

She was just beginning to doze off when a knock sounded on the window.

Kira cracked one eye open. "Colonel Kaen?"

"Good, you're awake. It's time we chat." He kept his gaze fixed on her as he passed through the containment tunnel into the room.

When the door hissed open, Kira tilted her head questioningly. "Sir, I thought you'd be in bed by now. It's late."

"Just wanted to check on you." Kaen stopped at the foot of her bed. "Since it's just the two of us, no need for all the formality."

Maybe Doctor Elric is onto something. This doesn't sound like the colonel at all. "I appreciate you stopping by." Not really, but Kira figured that's what people in her circumstances should say.

"When I sent you on that mission, I didn't expect events to unfold this way."

"Well, a lot of things didn't go according to plan."

"I have to say, though, when things don't work out like you envision, that's when you learn a lot about yourself as a leader. I've learned more about myself in the last few days than I ever knew I could."

Kira grunted. "Aside from what happened to me, things didn't go *that* badly. We still took down the lab and got the woman behind it all."

Kaen frowned. "Yes, though that was quite unfortunate she met such an untimely end."

"I'm sorry, sir, I hadn't intended to take it that far—she wouldn't submit." Kira looked down. "Not that sparing her life would have changed present circumstances, since she'd already dosed me with the nanites."

"Speaking of which," Kaen walked slowly along the side of the bed, "have you experienced any other transformations?"

"Nope, just been relaxing here."

"Perhaps you should try? There's no way to master new skills without practice."

"Yeah, I don't think that's really advisable in this case."

Kaen stopped midway along the bed near her knees. "Have you ever talked with other Gifted people?"

"Not really, no. Why?"

"Hmm, that's surprising."

Kira shrugged as much as she could in the restraints. "Valtan telepathy isn't held in very high regard among the telekinetically Gifted throughout the rest of the Taran worlds. I've never had the opportunity to interact with anyone, since the TSS turned me away."

"Well," the colonel continued, "I've heard secondhand there's a moment when someone first uses their abilities where it's so new and scary that the power is terrifying, overwhelming. Except, using those abilities is a fundamental part of their identity. It's only by pushing through the fear that they are able to come into their full selves."

"Except I wasn't born this way—I didn't choose to be a Robus. What happened to me is the product of illegal nanotech experimentation, end of story."

"Many advancements are an accident. History shows that those who seize opportunity hold the power."

Kira studied Kaen. She took a slow breath, trying to seem like she was considering his words. "Maybe this nanotech will turn out to be a helpful upgrade, but it's going to take time for me to adjust to the idea. I hope you'll be patient with me."

Kaen looked like he was going to say something else, his face tensing around his eyes and lips. After five seconds, he nodded. "Of course. Sleep well." He stiffly exited the room.

What in the stars is going on with him? Kira sunk into her pillows. *And what does he want from me?*

— — —

Something was most definitely off. Sandren watched Kaen storm out from the infirmary after his brief chat with Kira. *The man I've served under for the past decade wouldn't stop by just to check in on someone, no matter their condition. He's always been strictly business. Unless…*

Sandren would never get answers watching from a distance. He walked through the darkened infirmary to the quarantine area at the back. Kira's eyes were closed, but she was restless on the bed.

"Kira?" he asked softly through the comm at the window.

Her eyes flew open. "Who— Oh, Major. What are you…?"

"I saw Kaen was here. May we speak?"

"Yes, please!" She sat up in the bed as much as she could.

Sandren went through the tunnel and approached her. "How are you feeling?"

"Fine, sir. No other random transformations."

"And what did Kaen want?"

Kira bit her lower lip. "It's strange. Multiple times today, he's talked about me embracing this change. He wants me to learn to control it."

"What you told me before is looking more likely," Sandren admitted.

Kira looked him in the eyes. *"If he's listening to this…"*

Sandren submitted to her telepathic link. *"Clearly we're on the same page here."*

"Do you have a plan?"

Sandren shook his head. *"Not yet, but I'm working on it."*

"Do you think he's reporting to the same boss as Monica was? If they were working together, it would explain how she got away."

"A connection is likely. But what that connection is, I'm not sure yet."

Kira frowned. "I really don't know what to do about these modifications."

Sandren wasn't sure if the statement was genuine or if it was for the good of Kaen potentially listening in on their conversation. "The decision is yours, Kira, assuming they are able to come up with a countermeasure. If you want to keep the nanites, we'll adapt—provided they don't pose a security or health risk. If you want to go back to the way things were, no one will question it."

"I'd be lying if I denied there being some appeal to being physically powerful like the others on my team."

"Brute strength isn't the only kind of power."

She shrugged. "I know. But I *am* out in the field. It'd come in handy."

"You're actually considering this?"

"Something Kaen just told me rang true. Any change is scary, but I don't know what I can do or how this will affect me unless I give it a try."

Sandren nodded. "As long as you're under my command, I'll support whatever decision you make. We can seal off one of the sparring rooms and you can test out your new form, if you'd like."

Kira cracked a smile. "Thank you, sir."

CHAPTER 6

THE MTECH LAB looked untouched since Leon had last seen it three days prior, with the exception of the Mysaran landing craft no longer occupying the employee parking lot. The Guard landing shuttle set down at the end of the lot closest to the lab.

"It's so weird. I feel like I was *just* here," Ari jested.

"Yeah, yeah, I know." Leon hopped out of the landing shuttle and stretched.

It'd been a long day of travel on the *Raven* and it felt great to be on solid land again. *Only three days and I'm already missing being planetside.* Not a great start for his new Guard career in space.

The soldiers opened up the back of the shuttle to prep it for their mission. Though the craft wasn't a cargo vessel, the equipment Leon was after should fit in the rear cargo area that was typically reserved for mission-specific tech and armaments. Each team member wore standard body armor and carried a multi-handgun, but with any luck, even those wouldn't come into play.

Wearing armor felt strange to Leon after spending his

whole career in either business clothes or a lab coat. He had no interest in being in the middle of combat, but he'd certainly rather spend time in awkward attire than have a gaping hole through his chest.

"You don't think anyone from MTech has come back here, do you?" Leon asked the group.

"No signs I can see from here," Ari replied. "If you're wondering about why we're wearing armor, it's because we never go anywhere unprotected. We'd be in powered armor if we thought we were going to face opposition."

"I do have to say, it's much nicer here on Valta when I'm not being shot at," Nia said with a grin.

Kyle rolled his eyes. "You're not kidding anyone, Nia. You love a good firefight."

She placed a hand on her hip. "A *good* firefight, yes, which is one I've already won. If the enemy is still shooting, or hasn't even started yet, there's nothing good about that!"

Ari rolled a hovercart out of the shuttle. "I think most people would say they're in it for the win."

"Except maybe the Mysarans," Kyle replied. "Or it seems that way since they never do."

Leon frowned at the man. "Let's just focus on the mission."

The soldier straightened. "Sorry, I didn't mean to touch a nerve."

"Look, I know Elusia is in the Empire now and Mysar is still on the outside, but Valta has equal ties to both worlds. I went to grad school on Mysar. I have nothing against the people themselves," Leon explained.

Nia patted Kyle on his shoulder. "In other words, we should all try to get along and be civil. Come on."

The four of them traversed the path from the parking area to the ruined entryway of the lab. Plastic sheeting was affixed to the building frame to seal the openings where windows had been shot out during the firefight. Stone fragments and glass shards littered the walkway and flowerbeds around the entrance.

"Glad I wasn't in the middle of this," Leon murmured.

Ari shrugged. "It wasn't as bad as it seems from this aftermath."

"Still, I'm looking forward to getting back to our roots with covert entry," Nia said.

"With you there!" Kyle agreed. "Darting through the shadows, hacking into computer networks."

She smiled. "That's the life."

When they reached the plastic sheeting, Ari produced a utility knife from a belt pouch and sliced a slit down and along the bottom edge to create a diagonal flap. He slipped through the opening with the hover cart and activated a light mounted to the front of his tactical vest.

"Yeah, doesn't look like anyone's been in here," he announced. "Come on in."

The rest of the team followed him.

Kyle crouched at the entrance and set a small electronic device on the floor.

"What's that?" Leon asked.

"Sensor," the soldier replied. "If anyone comes inside, we'll get an alert."

"That's rather handy." Leon led the way toward A Wing on the right side of the lobby.

The A Wing security arch had fared better than the one to B Wing, but with the power disconnected from the building, it was just lifeless ornamentation.

Leon clicked on his own chest light as they approached the double-doors leading into the wing, which were still propped open from the prior infiltration.

The stark white corridor was downright creepy in the dark stillness. Leon listened for anything moving in the shadows, but the place was empty. He tried to shake the feeling that they were being watched—well aware of how many security cameras had been watching him every day at work before—but he knew that was silly.

They reached the lab where Leon had conducted the bulk of his research before the Guard raid. With a pang in his chest, he saw the family pictures still on his coworkers' desks.

"When do you think people will be allowed to gather their things?" he asked.

"Tough call," Nia replied. "The Guard has been talking with MTech about what went on here, but I don't know the details. I imagine whenever they reach an accord, MTech will get the facility back, and it'll be up to them who they let in, if anyone."

"Tribeca was counting on this lab being part of the local economy." Leon shook his head. "Shame it had to be mothballed."

"It could still re-open," Kyle pointed out. "If the Guard determines that MTech isn't corrupted at its core, then the honest workers like you will be able to get right back to what they were doing—the good parts."

"Yeah, I guess." Leon set aside the thoughts about his former coworkers and started running through his mental inventory of the items they needed to retrieve. "It'll be a tight fit on that cart, but I think we can grab everything in one trip."

"Good, because I can't say I'm fond of this place." Nia poked at the arm of a task light mounted to the island workstation at the center of the room.

"All right, we need to grab this bioconverter," Leon said as he walked across the room to a freestanding piece of equipment a meter and a half tall and a meter wide and deep. "It's heavy."

Ari leaned against the device and it barely rocked up on its back edge. "Yeah, no shite."

"We'll get it together." Kyle got situated on one side with Ari on the other.

With a grunt, the two men scooted the device forward a centimeter.

"Okay, so it's not exactly mobile," Ari wheezed.

"Sorry. I can help," Leon offered.

"No, no, we've got it," Kyle said as he and Ari muscled the equipment forward again. They tipped it on its back edge to get the front over the lip of the hovercart. "1… 2… 3!"

They heaved it up, the cart dipping momentarily while the hover controls adjusted to the weight change. The two soldiers slid the bioconverter to the back of the cart to make room for more.

"Good job. What else?" Nia asked.

"You're not going to like this, either." Leon directed the three soldiers through the lab, grabbing two more oversized items and a number of smaller tools he figured would be easier to take rather than procuring elsewhere. Frankly, he didn't care if MTech ever got the equipment back, even if it was legally their property.

When the hovercart was loaded down, Leon made a final circuit of the room to make sure they had everything he'd need.

His gaze rested on his office. "Mind if I grab one more thing?"

"If it's small and you can carry it yourself, go for it," Ari said.

Leon jogged over to his desk. Placed on the corner was the

statue he'd received as a graduation gift from his parents. The metal planet sat atop a square pedestal. While it had no commercial value, the gift had come at a time when Leon wasn't sure where life would lead him, and his parents had said the whole universe was his for the taking. He'd attached those words to the statue and had vowed to find himself the life he'd dreamed about. Even though that life was now in space, he'd still have this planet to remind him of home.

"That it?" Ari asked.

"Yep, ready to go." Leon nodded.

"Okay, let's—" Kyle cut off. "Well, that just figures."

"What?" questioned Nia.

Kyle consulted a screen mounted to the underside of his wrist. "We have company."

CHAPTER 7

LEON SWORE UNDER his breath. The last thing they needed were trespassers giving them a hard time while the Guard team tried to leave the lab with a cart full of irreplaceable equipment. "Who's here?"

Kyle reviewed the details on his wrist read-out. "Looks like vibration signatures for two individuals on the sensor I left by the front door."

"Not an army, at least," Nia muttered.

"No, but that doesn't mean they can't hurt us," Ari replied, readying his handgun on the sonic stun setting. "Let's move the cart closer to the entry and find a secure location to leave it. Then we can see who's out there."

Nia nodded, drawing her own handgun. She led the way down the hall with Kyle while Ari pushed the hovercart.

When they neared the door to the lobby, they turned off the lights on their armor.

"Let me get the cart," Leon suggested. "I haven't practiced much with guns."

Ari nodded and stepped aside for Leon to take over. The

soldier drew his weapon and shimmied around the cart to join his teammates.

"Any guesses on who they might be?" Nia whispered.

"Could be anyone from MTech officials to curious locals," Kyle replied. "MTech is more likely, but I really hope it's the latter."

They ran their hands along the wall for guidance in the near-blackness. Half a dozen meters from the exit, they directed Leon to park the cart.

Nia, Kyle, and Ari crept forward down the hall. They gestured for Leon to stay back, but he was curious to see who'd come to the lab. He followed them forward with his handgun at the ready, hoping he wouldn't have to use it.

Ari passed by the others and pressed his back against the side wall. "All right, I can make out two figures, as expected," he whispered to the team. "Doesn't look like they have on armor—or, at least not powered armor."

"We can easily take on two, if we have to," Nia whispered.

"They're just standing in the middle of the lobby talking," Ari relayed. "I can't hear them from here."

"Can you listen in using the sensor?" Leon asked.

Nia shook her head. "We could in our powered armor, but we don't have the right comm setup here."

"They're still talking," Ari reported.

Kyle looked back over his shoulder to Leon and Nia. "Do we wait it out or announce ourselves?"

"This place is under a Guard-instituted lockdown, so we have every right to be here. I say we step forward but leave the cart for now," Nia replied.

"Sounds good to me." Kyle stood up. "Wait here until we give the all clear, Leon."

Leon nodded, pressing his back against the side wall. He

inched forward with the soldiers until he had a view of the lobby and then stopped to observe.

"Hello!" Kyle called as he turned on his suit's light. His weapon was drawn, but he had it pointed down. "What can we do for you?"

The two figures in the lobby came to attention.

"Who are you?" the first asked in a mid-range voice that could be male or female. Leon couldn't make out any distinguishing physical features in the dim light shining through the plastic sheeting.

"We're representatives from the Guard," Kyle said. "Per the notice posted outside, this site is under active Guard investigation."

"We need to ask you to leave," the second figure stated in a lower male voice.

"Please identify yourselves," Ari requested as he stepped forward to join Kyle.

"You have no authority here," the first person replied.

"Actually, we do." Kyle tensed, raising his weapon the slightest measure. "State your name and business."

The second person scoffed. "Get out of here and leave us alone."

"Can't do that." Ari raised his weapon.

Nia took the opportunity to join in. "Hey, guys, what seems to be the trouble?"

"These trespassers don't want to play nice," Kyle told her.

"Trespassers?" The second person laughed. "We can't trespass on our own property."

"You're MTech?" Nia prompted.

"Probably easiest for you to think of us that way, yes." The first person said. "And we're here to assess this foking mess you made of our investment."

"That will have to wait until after the investigation is complete," Kyle said. "Please leave."

"No," the first person said. They took a step forward into the illumination cast by Kyle's light, highlighting an ageless feminine face with pale green eyes framed by dark hair.

Leon's heart skipped a beat. *Fok! That's the Mysaran chancellor!*

The voice was so familiar now that he'd identified her. The man, though, he couldn't place. It was possible he was somehow connected to MTech and out of the public eye.

But why is the Mysaran chancellor here on Valta in a condemned MTech lab? He needed to make sure the Guard team knew who she was. Or, maybe it was better for her to think she'd remained anonymous.

Shite, what do I do? Leon stood against the wall, paralyzed with indecision. He ran through the most likely scenarios and decided he couldn't just stand by and do nothing—not after what MTech had done to his home. If the Mysaran government had a hand in that, they didn't deserve any degree of anonymity or excuse.

Leon took a deep breath and stepped out from the shadows, turning on his light. "Madam Chancellor, please forgive my companions. They aren't from this system."

The chancellor came to attention. "Then you must be."

The Guard soldiers dropped the aim of their weapons.

"A Valtan native," Leon confirmed, "but I went to school on Mysar."

"As many do." She evaluated him. "But now you align yourself with the Taran Empire?"

"I aim to serve my people in the best way I can, and I have deemed that to be through service to the Guard, now that this MTech lab has been exposed for what it was. Ma'am," he added as an afterthought.

"Oh, so you worked here?" The man's dark brown eyes looked Leon over, and his lip curled under a moustache.

"I'm a research scientist. I know what went on here, and I'll keep working with the Guard to make sure no one else falls victim to the inhumane research practices that were happening here behind the scenes."

The chancellor turned to her male companion. "You hear that? It was *inhumane*."

He chuckled. "What a quaint interpretation."

Kyle raised his weapon again. "I don't care who you are. No one talks about what happened at this site like it was okay. Not on my watch. Now why are you here?"

"We already told you: to inspect," the chancellor stated. "The Mysaran government has significant holdings in MTech, and it's our right to audit our assets."

"Not buying it," Nia said. "Sorry, ma'am."

"You're making a mistake by trying to detain us," the man said.

Ari squinted. "I dunno. We're not the ones with guns pointed in our faces."

The chancellor chuckled. "What, you think we'd come alone?"

The plastic over the building opening billowed with a gust of wind outside. The low rumble of an engine vibrated the structure.

"We're here to reclaim our equipment," the man said. "If you refuse to leave, I'll have you forcibly removed."

Leon took a step back toward the A Wing corridor. *I need to get that cart.*

"Where do you think you're going?" the chancellor asked.

"Consider it my severance package." Leon ran across the lobby.

Before he'd gone four steps, a heavy form slammed into his back, knocking him to the ground.

The air was forced from his lungs as he landed heavily.

An arm looped around his neck. "Should have walked away when you had the chance."

Leon gasped for air as the arm tightened around him. Mind racing, he clawed at the man, but he didn't have the strength to overpower him.

Then, Leon spotted his globe figurine out of the corner of his eye. He snatched the base from next to him and drove the point of the pedestal backward.

The man cried out in pain and released Leon.

Coughing, and with a hand on his throat, Leon grabbed the globe part of the figurine and scrambled across the floor away from the man. When he looked back, he saw the man holding a hand over his right eye where he'd been struck by the point.

Leon was about to smash the man's head with the metal sphere of the globe when he remembered he had the stun gun. He tucked the figurine into his vest and then trained the weapon on the man. "Who are you?"

"It doesn't matter. You won't be around long enough to tell anyone."

Leon pulled the trigger, and a sonic wave swept over the man. He fell limp on the ground.

A quick check over his shoulder confirmed that Ari, Kyle, and Nia had the chancellor subdued, so Leon made a run for the hovercart they'd left in the hall.

He activated the controls on the back and pushed it forward at its top speed—barely above a walking tempo with it so weighed down.

Ari ran over to help push it. "Sorry! We couldn't shoot him without knocking you out, too."

"I'm not completely helpless." Leon leaned into the cart.

"This isn't going fast enough." Ari stopped pushing. "We need to get out of here before whoever it is coming down in that ship shows up!"

"We can't leave this here!"

Ari hesitated. "It'll help Kira?"

"I hope so."

The soldier nodded. "Okay, bring it as quickly as it will go. I'll scout ahead and try to hold them off with the others." Ari ran toward the entrance.

Leon lay into the hovercart and willed it along. *This isn't the time for technology to fail me.*

Ahead, the sound of pounding footsteps echoed through the lobby as the three soldiers ran to get into position. Leon peeked around the bin to see them duck through the slit in the plastic sheeting.

The chancellor and her companion were still passed out on the floor. Leon wished they had time to interrogate them, but there was no chance.

Finally, he made it to the plastic sheeting. When he tried to push the cart through, though, the top snagged on the upper flap of the triangular opening. He attempted to force it through, but the heavy plastic didn't want to rip under the minimal thrust the hovercart was able to muster while weighed down.

Leon dug through the pouches on his belt looking for a utility knife. He found one in a compartment on his left hip and frantically cut away the extra plastic to fit the cart through.

Just as he finished, gunshots sounded in the direction of the parking lot. The three Guard soldiers were nowhere to be seen.

Ari ducked around the corner of the building back into

Leon's view. "Leave the cart! We have to go *now!*"

"But—"

"It's about survival now." Ari ran back around the corner and joined in the exchange of kinetic rounds.

Leon took one final look at the stack of equipment and then left it behind to join his team. He'd be no help to Kira if he were dead.

He slowly approached the corner where he'd last seen Ari and peeked around. The team members were hiding behind landscaping features that provided minimal cover from a group of two dozen enemy soldiers.

Oh shite! How are we supposed to make it back to the shuttle? Leon unholstered his handgun. He was barely comfortable shooting while standing still, let alone use it while running for his life. "I'm here! What do we do?" he called to his team just loud enough to be heard.

"Shuttle is on its way," was Kyle's only response.

Leon spotted the landing shuttle making its way over to the team. He located a likely landing spot only fifteen meters from the main door to the building.

"Back it up," Leon called back. "I can make a straight shot with the cart. That equipment is why we came here."

"Do it," Nia said without taking her eyes off the approaching enemies.

Leon dashed to where he'd left the cart in the doorway.

Inside, he saw the chancellor and her companion beginning to stir, so he gave them another shot with his handgun after confirming it was on the stun setting.

He swung around the back of the cart and began pushing it forward at its pathetic top speed. It tore through the weakened plastic sheeting, and he made a straight run for where the shuttle would supposedly land.

Weapons fire continued just around the corner.

"They're close enough!" Kyle yelled, and the low boom of the sonic blasters sounded.

Kinetic gunfire ceased, and Kyle, Ari, and Nia barreled toward Leon.

Together, they pushed the cart forward, their combined strength driving it forward faster than it could handle on its own power.

The shuttle descended from the sky in front of them, its back hatch falling open moments before the group reached the ramp.

They pushed the cart inside, and Kyle was at the controls in a matter of seconds.

Leon gripped a handhold next to the door as the shuttle lifted off the ground while the back hatch was still closing.

"That was way too close." He leaned against the wall as the hatch sealed.

"We're lucky they tried to advance on us—couldn't fire the pulse guns at the distance they were before." Nia took a deep breath. "Did we get everything?"

"I think so." Leon checked over the cart. It looked good.

"Shouldn't have gone back like that," Ari said. "If we hadn't been able to knock them out at the last second, you would have been shot to bits on that run."

Leon stared him down. "I came here to complete a mission. That's precisely what I was doing."

Kyle cracked a smile. "We might make a Guard soldier out of you yet."

CHAPTER 8

IF THERE WAS anything President Joris couldn't stand, it was inaction. He drummed his fingers on his desktop, trying to suppress his frustration about Colonel Kaen's dismissive response to his warning regarding Chancellor Hale.

How could he not take this threat seriously? The Mysaran military might be nothing compared to the Taran Empire's forces, but they're only hours from Elusia! Don't they want to protect us? After all, that was the impetus for Elusia rejoining the Empire. If Joris didn't get backup when he needed it, what was the point?

He rose from his chair and paced across the office, hoping to clear his head. Worry clouded his judgment, and he needed to maintain rational thought in order to be a good leader.

But, a good leader would go out of his way to protect his people, even if it meant being forceful.

No taking 'no' for an answer. With his mind made up, Joris returned to his desk to open a secure subspace comm link with Guard headquarters. *I'll talk to Kaen directly if he won't take action on his own.*

The call took almost a minute to connect. Colonel Kaen appeared on the holodisplay hovering above the president's desk. "President Joris, what may I do for you?"

"Hello, Colonel. I wanted to follow up regarding that message I sent you the other day."

Kaen frowned. "Like I said, I'm looking into it."

"Well, Colonel, that's not good enough for me. I need assurances that this matter will be investigated swiftly and thoroughly."

"With all respect, Mr. President, that isn't your demand to make."

Joris bristled. "Elusia is now a full member of the Taran Empire, and we are facing an immediate threat within our system. Mysaran forces can reach us in a matter of hours, and I have reason to believe that their chancellor is under outside influence and intends to harm Elusia. 'Looking into it' on your own timeframe won't work."

"Just because your planet is now in the Empire doesn't mean you get free rein to direct our resources. It's my responsibility to determine the most urgent threats and allocate our forces accordingly. Right now, you're not the top priority."

"Then I'd like to speak with the general in charge of your base."

Kaen chuckled. "Mr. President, if you think going over my head will help your case, you're sorely mistaken."

That's it? We're on our own? Joris stared levelly at the colonel. "This isn't the attitude I'd expect from an officer in the Guard."

"Then perhaps you need to reset your expectations." Kaen ended the call.

Joris leaned back in his chair and scoffed. It was like he was talking to an entirely different person than the man he'd worked with in the previous months regarding the MTech investigations. *Unless...*

His pulse spiked. "Ellen!" he called over the intercom. "Come up here right away."

"On my way, sir," she acknowledged.

She arrived less than two minutes later. "Sir, what is it?"

"I may know why the Guard didn't act on our information."

Ellen took a seat across from Joris. "Why?"

"I have nothing more than a hunch to go on, but it's possible that Colonel Kaen is under the same influence as Chancellor Hale."

"Stars!" Ellen's face drained. "Are they working together?"

"Maybe not together, but possibly for the same side." Joris spread his hands on the desktop. "Whatever's going on, they don't want others butting in."

"Then that's exactly what we have to do."

The president evaluated her. "That's a dangerous proposition. If someone as high-ranking as Kaen has been subverted, and hasn't been caught, then he has authority to take actions that could easily wipe us out. Having the Guard as an enemy would be exponentially worse than the Mysarans."

"But we're members of the Empire now!"

"Yes, but if Elusia is declared a threat? They'd just as soon turn against us."

Ellen crossed her arms. "We're trapped."

"No, we just have to get creative," Joris replied. "It's time you reach out to your brother. There has to be someone in the Guard who'll help us."

— — —

The landing shuttle ascended at a steep angle through Valta's sky toward its rendezvous with the *Raven*. Leon remained standing next to the hovercart, as the shuttle was too small for him to shimmy around it to get to his seat.

Once in space, the shuttle maneuvered to the underbelly of the *Raven* and slipped into its berth. The hatch dropped open once they were safely inside.

"I'll get this into storage." Leon directed the cart down the ramp toward the cargo area.

Nia followed him. "Despite what Ari said, we're all happy you went back for it. The mission comes first, especially since it's for Kira."

"I'll do right by her," he said.

"Good." Nia backed away and formed a 'V' with her index and middle fingers, pointing them to her eyes, and then to Leon. "Because we're watching you." She smiled and climbed the ladder with the other soldiers.

Leon shook his head and chuckled as he strapped the cart to the cargo bay's grated deck. When he was finished, he climbed the ladder to the common area. The members of Kira's team were nowhere to be seen, but Gil and Sven were on the couch again.

"Hi," Leon greeted.

"Oh, hey." Sven pointed upward. "You got a call while you were down on the surface."

"From whom?"

"Dunno." Sven shrugged.

Curious, Leon climbed the ladder and headed for his cabin. He'd made it three meters down the hall when someone called his name from behind.

Leon turned to see a woman descending from the bridge.

"I'm Aleya, the first officer of the *Raven*," she greeted. "You had an urgent call from Elusia. We said you'd call back when you were on board."

"Who was it?" Leon asked as he walked toward her.

"Your sister, Ellen."

"Ellen? Why would she be calling me here?" Leon wondered aloud.

"It was important enough that they routed it to us. Said she'd only talk to you. We have a private communications booth up on the flight deck." Aleya scaled the ladder.

"Thanks." Leon followed her.

The upper level of the *Raven* was more compact than the residential and rec levels below, as it was housed inside a protrusion at the top of the vessel. The ladder led to one end of a central corridor. To the right, toward the nose of the vessel, a door sealed off the bridge. To the aft, a small social area was on one side of the corridor, complete with a booth and table, and beyond were doors to enclosed rooms.

Aleya indicated the first room. "Comm system is all set up for you. Sister said you'd know her direct line."

"Thank you." Leon inclined his head and went into the booth. The space was only two meters square, but it was equipped with a holodisplay and two padded seats. He sat down and entered in Ellen's contact information on Elusia.

She answered after twenty seconds. "Leon, thanks for getting back to me so quickly."

"I was on an op. What's so urgent?"

"You... on an op?"

"Yeah, it's a long story." Leon shook his head, not wanting to explain what was going on with Kira, if he even could. "So, why'd you call?'

"I wanted to follow up regarding a message President Joris sent Colonel Kaen."

Leon crossed his arms. "I wouldn't know anything about that."

"No, but you're close to Kira, and Kira is in Kaen's chain-of-command, right?"

"Yes, but it's not like she can just ask about his private conversations with the president," Leon pointed out. *Not to mention the suspicions that Kaen isn't himself.* Yet another thing he didn't want to explain to Ellen.

"Well, we relayed a rather important piece of information, and it's being dismissed—even to President Joris' face."

Leon's breath caught. "And this only went to Colonel Kaen?"

"Yes."

Shite. Leon leaned back in the chair and sighed. "If Kaen didn't act on the information, then he had a reason." *And the information didn't match with the goals of whatever influence he's under.*

His sister eyed him. "Leon, do you know something?"

"What is this information, anyway?" Leon hedged.

She swallowed. "Is this communication encrypted?"

Leon checked the details of the comm link. It would route through Guard headquarters, which meant there'd be a record someone of Kaen's rank could access. "Not well enough," he told her. "But the fact that we've already had this much of the conversation won't make a difference."

Ellen nodded. "We told Kaen that the Mysaran Chancellor might be under some kind of influence."

That explains what she was doing on Valta today. Well, part of it. Leon groaned. "There are people I can trust. I'll pass on the message."

— — —

Kira couldn't take being strapped down any longer. *Getting agitated will only make it more likely I transform. I need to work off this energy more productively.*

She took a calming breath and pressed the call button they'd placed near her right hand. "Doctor Elric, may we have a word?"

"I'll be right there, Kira." The doctor entered through the tunnel three minutes later. "Is everything all right?"

"No," Kira admitted. "I don't think being strapped down here is the answer. I thought I might keep transforming randomly, but there hasn't been so much as an eye glow since that incident soon after I arrived in the infirmary."

"What are you suggesting?"

"Let me use one of the sparring rooms. Put four guards at the door. If I transform and lose control, they can subdue me with a sonic blast."

The doctor considered the request. "I don't have any medical grounds to hold you in quarantine. Those safety measures seem appropriate for the circumstances."

Kira perked up. "I can go?"

"I know Colonel Kaen would approve, so I don't see why not."

She looked into the doctor's eyes and asked telepathically, *"Why did you tell me Kaen isn't who he seems?"*

Elric hesitated. *"We shouldn't talk about it here."*

"This telepathic link is the most secure communication there is. Tell me. Pretend like you're giving me an exam."

He took an unsteady breath and began checking Kira's limbs, making eye contact on occasion to maintain the telepathic link. *"He thinks I don't remember, but I do."*

"Remember what?"

"Right before you came for your medical check-up, after

getting home from Valta, Kaen came to see me," the doctor explained. *"He told me to delete the test results showing your new nanites and to forget I saw anything—or that I'd even talked to him. And I did, until I saw you transform. The memories slowly came back until I realized what the colonel had done."*

Kira's heart skipped a beat as she thought through the implications of the revelation. *"Have you been able to test him?"*

"No. I didn't want to give any indication that I suspected something was amiss," the doctor replied. *"I have no idea what he might do to us if he learned we were discussing it now."*

"We have to go to someone about this," Kira urged. *"Major Sandren. I trust him with my life, especially with my current state."*

"Whatever happened to the colonel, it must be recent. He's always been a reliable member of the Guard."

"I've never doubted him, either, but something has been off since the Valta op…"

"The ability to exert telepathic orders—especially to alter memory—isn't something he should be able to do," the doctor added.

"What could enable that kind of skill?"

"I can't think of a single thing that we have access to within the Guard. That's the TSS' area of expertise."

"Do you think the TSS or its Agents are involved?"

"No, they've always stopped *this kind of subversion. The closest incident was a neurotoxin first used by the Bakzen and later adapted by the Priesthood."*

Kira raised one of her arms for the doctor to fake-examine. *"Could some survivors from the Priesthood be behind this?"*

"Unlikely—none of the other facts line up. Given how even our advanced scans can't readily detect any issues, that suggests this is something we haven't encountered before."

"*Any theories?*" Kira prompted.

"*Against all odds, it might be alien,*" the doctor asserted.

"*That would align with what we learned from MTech.*"

"*Are the nanites and the method of telepathic subversion from the same alien source? I can't be certain,*" Elric continued. "*Either way, it's alarming to think about MTech having access to alien technology the Taran Empire hasn't seen before.*"

"*No shite.*" Kira sighed inwardly. "*I'll meet with Major Sandren as soon as I can. We'll figure out what's going on with Kaen.*"

The doctor nodded and broke the telepathic connection. "No further symptoms, Kira. I think that workout you requested is just what you need."

"Thank, you, Doctor."

"I'll arrange an escort to the training room for you." The doctor departed.

Kira sat in quiet contemplation for the next twenty minutes, thinking about the opponents she'd encountered in missions over her decade-long career. Though rare, people with telepathic and telekinetic abilities would occasionally make an appearance, but those abilities were always innate traits. For someone to be possessed by another sentient presence was a whole new situation. She couldn't think of an explanation.

A new alien foe. Well, that's fantastic. She groaned. It was shaping up to be quite the week.

Her thoughts were interrupted by a complement of guards arriving outside the containment chamber.

"Captain Elsar," the largest of the four guards said, "we've been directed by Doctor Elric to take you to one of the sparring rooms for physical training."

"I'm thrilled to hear it, Private," Kira replied. "Have you

been apprised of my condition?"

"Yes, ma'am. We're prepared for any contingency." He patted a sonic handgun on his hip.

"All right. Now get me out of here!" Kira smiled and jangled her restraints.

The four soldiers entered. Two cautiously released her restraints while the other two stood by with their sonic pistols at the ready. Kira had to admit it was a disconcerting change to be on the receiving end of a weapon in close quarters.

When the final cuff was disconnected from the bed, the soldiers directed Kira to her feet and placed stasis cuffs on her for the walk down to the sparring room.

"My friends are going to wonder what kind of crazy shenanigans I got into over the weekend to end up being escorted by you guys," Kira jested as they bound her wrists behind her back with stasis cuffs.

"I bet we could come up with an epic story if you'd like, ma'am," the lead guard offered.

She grinned. "Nothing yet. We should keep people guessing. Helps with my mystique."

They led her from the containment chamber and through the infirmary. Workout facilities were located near the residential sections of headquarters but also in designated team training areas within the outer reaches of the facility. They headed to one of the lesser-used areas to minimize the number of potentially prying eyes, not knowing if she might transform.

As they worked their way through the facility, she found herself questioning whether or not she *wanted* to transform. As frightening as the prospect was, she was curious about what she might be able to do. All the same, she recognized that Colonel Kaen wanted her to do just that, and following the advice of a potentially subverted individual under unknown alien control was undoubtedly a bad move.

By the time they reached the entrance of the designated sparring room, Kira had decided to fight the transformation to the best of her ability. If Kaen wanted her to gain mastery, then the opposite course of action was what she needed to do.

The guards ushered her inside the six-by-six meter chamber, which had pads arranged on the floor in the center of the space and various weapons and other training implements along the side walls, including racks of free-weights.

"Give me forty-five minutes," Kira told the guards.

"Yes, ma'am." The lead guard undid Kira's stasis cuffs and then went to wait in the hall with his colleagues.

Kira grabbed some weights off the rack and began her usual rep routine. It felt great to get her blood moving after sitting nearly stationary for two days. She moved on to body weight exercises and combat forms.

Twenty minutes into her exercise, Kira noticed something was off. The weights and movements that were historically her most challenging were coming to her easily. She looked in the mirror on the back wall of the room, but she appeared normal—no glowing eyes, even. *Is this like the strength my teammates always seem to have?*

It was entirely possible she just had excess energy after doing nothing for days. She was about to continue the workout when one of the guards poked her head into the room.

"Ma'am, we were just informed that Leon Calleti is back. He wants to see you."

CHAPTER 9

COLONEL KAEN PACED across his office against his conscious will. It was curious that the being controlling him, despite not having a body of its own, liked to pace as it thought.

"They're onto us," Nox muttered in Kaen's mind.

"Onto you, *maybe,"* Kaen clarified. *"You haven't been doing a very good impersonation of me."*

"All your official procedures… it's wearisome."

Kaen made no indication, but Nox had inadvertently given him a gift. The alien had disclosed an annoyance, which presented a weakness for Kaen to exploit. He just had to find the right opportunity to use the Guard's regimented structure as a means to get him the help he needed. His unwanted tenant was about to get an eviction notice.

"Your interest in Kira will be your undoing," Kaen said, hoping to provoke a reaction. He had found that when Nox was emotional, the alien's grasp loosened.

Indeed, Nox's energy moved to the surface, giving Kaen room to flex within the inner recesses of himself.

"I am in control," Nox insisted.

"The Guard will come for you. They'll kill me rather than allow a subverted officer to live."

"Your people value individual lives too much to do that."

In reality, Kaen wasn't positive what would happen to him when he was inevitably found out, but he would rather die than compromise the Guard's security. He'd already caused enough inadvertent damage as it was. "They will kill me, and you'll die with me."

"This work is too important to abandon," Nox replied.

"You said Kira had to be delivered to your benefactors, though. How can you deliver her if you've been eliminated?"

Nox was silent for several seconds. "She must embrace her abilities. Someone must be here to give her guidance."

"Your presence won't make a difference either way. By remaining here, you're only putting yourself at risk," Kaen insisted. "As soon as they discover you inside me—which won't be long now since they already suspect—you'll either be removed or we'll both die. Neither option gets Kira wherever you want to take her."

"Then I will do a better job of blending in."

"The damage is already done." Kaen raised as much of a mental presence as he could muster. "If you want to succeed with this mission, then you have to run. Hide and wait for Kira to come into her own, then retrieve her."

"You're lying to me. You have your own intentions."

Kaen gave a mental shrug. "That's your call. I'm a prisoner in this body regardless."

"I suppose you would suggest the option that keeps you alive," Nox said.

"Of course. My own life is most important to me," Kaen lied.

"Then perhaps a change of plan is required."

"We'll need a ship," Kaen urged, shifting his language to promote a sense of team. Even faking it disgusted him, but he had no intention of letting the alien get its way. He'd play along just enough to get Nox in a vulnerable place.

"Will they let us go without a fight?"

"If we're quick," Kaen replied. *"Do you know somewhere safe to go?"*

"Yes, there is a place," Nox acknowledged. *"If you can get us out of here, I will take care of the rest."*

"Let me have control. I'll get the ship."

"No!" Nox swelled in his mind. *"Don't mistake my acceptance of your warnings for trust. I merely agree that it's not safe to remain here."*

"Then I'll tell you where to go," Kaen responded in a calm mental tone.

Kaen relayed the directions to Nox—first a list of items he'd need, since Nox tended to forget that Kaen required things like water, food, and clothing, and then directions for where to head with a travel bag. The plan wasn't up to the standards Kaen demanded of himself in the Guard, but he couldn't think about it too much, lest Nox discover his intentions.

The instructions entailed walking to one of the remote docking wings, like he was on official business, and then commandeering one of the craft. It was unclear where Nox planned to go from there, exactly, but that didn't matter to Kaen. If he had his way, they'd never make it off Orion Station.

Nox allowed Kaen to lead the way to the docking wing, though Kaen could tell his movements were being regulated.

He passed by several soldiers in the halls, and they nodded to him with respect. Despite Nox's annoyance, Kaen returned their gesture with nods of acknowledgment. Nox would know that's how he'd behave normally, and he needed to play the part.

As Kaen anticipated, the docking wing entrance was staffed by two guards at a reception desk.

"I need a transport ship for immediate departure," he ordered.

"Sir, no request has been filed," the first guard stated.

"I'm ordering you now," Kaen-Nox continued without missing a beat. "Direct me to a free vessel and I'll take care of the rest."

The two guards looked at each other, but they weren't in any position to question an order from a colonel, however irregular.

"The *Lisbeth II* is available," the second guard stated after consulting a monitor behind the desk. "Berth 23."

"Thank you." Kaen-Nox stepped through the doorway before the guards could ask for further clarification. His plan hinged on getting to the transport ship.

Beyond the door, a corridor branched in either direction. Airlock doors along the outer door led to gangways, which extended to the docked ships. Control panels next to each doorway indicated the docked vessel. Kaen-Nox continued to the left until he saw Berth 23 and double-checked that it held the *Lisbeth II*.

Kaen then used the control panel to enter dummy deployment orders, adding just enough detail to satisfy Nox's watchful eye, but the alien was unfamiliar with specifics of Guard policy. The moment any authorized personnel reviewed the orders, they'd know something was amiss.

"Are you finished yet?" Nox asked in an agitated tone within Kaen's mind.

"Do you want this done right or done fast?" he replied.

The alien backed down just the slightest measure.

Kaen finished inputting the dummy orders, and then cycled the airlock.

He stepped through, and the door sealed behind him. The ship was a straight shot down the gangway, viewports in the side walls revealing the vessel. The *Lisbeth II* and its sister ship were small craft suitable for little more than system-hopping on a day trip. However, it would serve Kaen's need just fine as a single passenger—not that he had any intention to go far.

"You do know how to operate this craft?" Nox asked.

"Of course. All officers receive basic flight training, but all these ships operate on autopilot, anyway."

It was a true statement, so Nox would never detect the lie hidden within. Operating the craft out in the open black was straightforward, but the undocking procedure was layered with tedious process—the kind of activities Nox seemed eager to overlook.

Once Kaen was on board, all he'd have to do was intentionally mess up a few commands and they'd lock him down, and then they'd see the error-riddled orders. Nox could take over control and say whatever he wanted, but there'd be no way to get out of the situation without a thorough med eval. It was Kaen's best chance to be freed from the prison within himself. With the plan tucked safely in the recesses of his innermost mind, he stepped aboard the *Lisbeth II*.

Kaen-Nox passed through the ship's airlock and cycled the inner door. He located the cockpit at the end of a short hallway to the left and took a seat in the command chair. He began powering up the craft.

"You're keeping something from me." Nox's words were accompanied with an icy vise around Kaen's mind.

"No, I'm—"

Kaen didn't have a chance to object. He was instantly

immobilized within himself, just as he had been when Nox first asserted itself. But this wasn't the time to admit defeat. Kaen had to fight it. This might be his only chance to make it out alive.

"*You'll never win!*" he shouted in his mind and lashed out toward Nox.

The alien was caught off-guard by the resistance as the two battled for control over Kaen's limbs. His right arm flailed in front of him, sweeping across the touch-panel for the ship's controls.

A hum filled the air as the engines revved, straining the ship against the docking clamps that were still engaged at the end of the gangway. They wouldn't hold for long.

— — —

Kira hurriedly stowed the free-weights she'd been using for her workout. *Did Leon get what he needed so he can figure out what in the stars is going on with me?*

She placed her wrists behind her back as she approached the waiting guards.

"Major Sandren instructed us to take you to a conference room where he and Leon will meet you," the guard said while cuffing her.

"Lead the way." Kira nodded to the door.

Five minutes later, Kira was deposited inside the conference room. It wasn't equipped for prisoner securement like an interrogation room, but the guards looped her cuffs through the support beams of the table, which was welded to the floor. Kira had to lean forward at an awkward angle, but it was still better than the confounded bed.

As the guards finished up, Major Sandren entered with

Leon right behind him.

Kira smiled. "Hello, sir. Welcome back, Leon."

"Hey." Leon looked like he wanted to run to her, but he restricted himself to a friendly smile in the major's presence.

"How'd it go on Valta?" Kira asked him.

"That's an interesting story. I asked Major Sandren to join us so I could explain what happened."

The major closed the door and adjusted some controls on the touch-panel mounted to the wall. "This room is secure. No one can listen in."

Leon nodded. "So, we got to Valta and everything started out fine. Equipment was loaded on a cart and we were on our way out. Then Kyle got an alert that two people had entered the MTech lobby."

"Who were they?" Major Sandren asked.

"That's why I was so insistent we meet. I have no idea who the man was, but I instantly recognized the woman as Chancellor Hale of the Mysaran Coalition."

Kira's breath caught in her throat. "The Mysaran Chancellor was touring a condemned MTech lab?"

"Precisely. Things got especially awkward when a group of well-armed soldiers showed up and started shooting at us." Leon frowned.

Sandren leaned back in his chair and released a long breath. "That confirms whatever MTech was up to had ties to the government."

"Yes, sir," Leon acknowledged, "but I'm afraid it might extend beyond Mysar."

"What makes you say that?" Sandren questioned.

"I talked to my sister after the op—she'd reached out while we were on the planet's surface. If you recall, she works for the Elusian president. They suspect Hale has been subverted, which fits with what I saw. However, President Joris had relayed this information to Kaen, and the colonel dismissed it. That makes sense, if what Doctor Elric suspects about Kaen is true."

Kira shook her head. "It's not just suspicion anymore. I've had enough weird conversations with him over the last two days to draw my own conclusions."

Major Sandren sat in quiet contemplation. "Kaen led the investigation into the recent security breach. It's possible some of the people involved were innocent and he pegged his own actions on them."

"I was just about to suggest the same thing, sir," Kira said.

The major nodded. "We need to detain Colonel Kaen. He has too much authority to remain free in this facility."

Kira's gaze passed between the major and Leon. "And you need to keep a close eye on me, too. Kaen came to speak with me and suggested that I embrace these Robus abilities. Whatever MTech was up to, I think modifying me was part of their plan, and Kaen's job might be to make sure I turn out how they hope."

Leon paled. "Kaen may have helped Monica escape."

"Or, at a minimum, not stopped her," Kira said. "In any case, the longer we talk here, the longer this base is in danger."

Sandren rose from the table. "I'll speak with General Lucian right away. And, Kira, as much as I want to trust you, I agree that it's too risky for you to be unsupervised until we understand exactly what was done to you. We can forgo the restraints, but I'd like you to stay on lockdown."

"Yes, sir, I understand." Not being lashed to the bed would at least be an upgrade. Though, she very well might wish she was strapped down on a bed if she had another seizure or whatever it was.

"Stand by for further instruction," Sandren ordered. "And it goes without saying that you speak of this to no one."

"Yes, sir," Kira and Leon both acknowledged.

The major left the room.

One of the guards entered. "Your cuffs, ma'am."

"Thanks." Kira rubbed her wrists as soon the guard removed the cuffs. "Give us another minute, Private."

"Yes, ma'am." The guard closed the door behind himself.

Kira took the opportunity to take Leon's hands. "I'm glad you made it back in one piece."

"Those MTech guys were trying hard to make sure that didn't happen." He shrugged it off. "Can't say I'm eager to be in combat again, though."

"I'm all for you being my scientist guy back here at base."

"That I can do." He leaned in and gave her a kiss. "And I need to get going on that testing."

"Yes, please tell me what's going on. I haven't had so much as an eye-glow in the last two days."

"There's no reason to believe there would be any kind of consistent expression of traits. It's actually surprising you were able to exercise any degree of control when you were on the verge of changing before."

"I hope you don't want me to intentionally change, because if that's what Kaen wants, it's probably the last thing I should do."

"We'll make that determination once I've completed a full model of your current genome and bloodwork."

Kira scowled at him. "Scientist you is so impersonal."

He smiled. "Rest assured, you'll be my favorite test subject."

"Yeah, well—"

An alarm interrupted Kira.

Leon jumped. "What's that for?"

"Nothing good."

— — —

Major Sandren stopped midstride when the alarm sounded. *The fok?*

He ran to the nearest control panel and entered his credentials to view the details for the alert. Someone was trying to force an override to release a transport ship from its grapple. If the alarm was sounding, that meant the station was at risk for a decompression.

What kind of idiot would be trying to launch a ship without disengaging the docking clamps? Sandren fumed.

No trained soldier, that's for sure. So, either someone had forgotten all their training or the pilot was under duress. Regardless of the reasons, that docking wing needed as many Guard personnel as possible to get the situation under control.

Sandren ran down the corridor.

CHAPTER 10

KIRA DASHED TO the conference room's exit. "We need to find out what that alarm is for."

"Should you be, you know, out and about?" Leon asked behind her.

She was torn. Feeling like herself at the moment didn't mean she wasn't actually under some form of influence. But, if there was an emergency situation, there was no way under the stars that she was going to be locked in a holding cell while the base was in crisis.

Kira looked over her shoulder at Leon. "Right now, the most pressing danger is whatever is causing that alarm." She opened the door and found the four guards waiting outside, looking concerned. "Private, any info about the alarm?"

"There's a notice about pressurization failure, but that's all I know, ma'am," one soldier replied.

The station might depressurize? Kira's heart leaped. They'd trained for that kind of emergency, but she never dreamed she'd have to put those skills to use. "We need to get to a control center."

"Ma'am, we're supposed to bring you back to Medical."

"Those orders came through before there was a foking alarm telling us we all might die!" Kira shot back.

"Uh…" Leon paled.

"Might be an exaggeration. Hopefully." Kira stared down the private barring her path. "I'll have the good doctor here to escort me," she said, gesturing toward Leon.

"Right, yes," Leon said to her relief.

"I'm… I'm not sure—"

"Private, the circumstances have changed. I'm not an enemy being detained; this was a voluntary isolation. Either let me go now or I'm going to force my way out."

The soldier reluctantly stepped aside, and his comrades parted.

"Thank you." Kira passed through the opening and headed to the left toward the nearest control room.

"You know I can't do squat to stop you if you lose control," Leon whispered when they were beyond earshot from the guards.

"It won't come to that."

Kira jogged down the hall with Leon close behind. The control room was around a corner a hundred meters from the conference room. She tried the door, but it was locked.

"Bomax," she muttered while fiddling with the controls on the touch-panel.

"Can you override it?"

"Yes, but it won't be easy. The depressurization warning has sealed all the doors."

"Yeah, again, that sounds like something I should be worried about!"

Kira ignored Leon's concerns for the time being, focusing on the task at hand. She couldn't make an informed assessment of their circumstances until she knew exactly what they were up against.

After a minute of trying various overrides for the door, she finally found an authorization that worked. The bolt unlocked with a satisfying *clang*, and then the door hissed open.

Kira dashed to the control panel on the back wall. She searched for details about the lockdown. "Oh, shite…"

Leon ran up next to her, examining the screen. "What is it?"

"A ship is trying to break away from the station while the docking clamps are still engaged. It'll rip a hole in this section if it gets free."

"Why would someone—"

"No one in their right mind would." Kira took a steadying breath. "Kaen."

"Kaen-Kaen or alien-Kaen?"

"For all I know it's a fight between the two of them."

Leon crossed his arms. "What do we do?"

"*You* are going to stay here. The room will remain pressurized even if the rest of this arm of the station loses atmosphere."

"Kira, no, you're not going up against—"

"I'll find Sandren or someone on my team."

Leon spread his arms. "You can't just leave me here!"

"I can't bring you along, either. I need to get to the colonel. No one else knows what's going on with him, so they'd be liable to either shoot him on sight or let him go," Kira insisted. "I need to help bring him in unharmed."

"And then what?"'

"You figure out how to get that thing out of him."

"Me?!"

"Hey, you signed up to be the Guard's greatest new scientific mind."

A flush crept into Leon's face. "Yeah, for *genetics* research! And let's not forget I'm already trying to solve what's going on with *you*."

"That can wait. The colonel needs our help, and fixing whatever happened to him means we might be able to help the Mysaran Chancellor, too."

"Kira—"

"I'll be fine. And you'll be safe here. Remember the safety briefing about your shipsuit, should you need to pressurize it." She gave him a quick kiss. "I'll be back as soon as I can."

Before Leon could object further, she ran out the door into the corridor. She resealed the door behind her.

The endangered docking wing was up two decks, so Kira ran to the nearest access ladder, knowing the lift would be locked. She scaled the rungs and then ran down the hall toward the docking location as soon as she reached the top.

Two bewildered guards stood behind the security desk at the wing's entrance.

"What's going on?" Kira demanded.

"Don't know, ma'am," one replied. "Colonel Kaen came by a few minutes ago, and then Sandren—"

The deck shuddered, accompanied by a groan of grating metal.

"Get yourselves to a safe place," Kira instructed. She opened the wing door. "Make sure this is sealed behind me." She ran through.

The sound of grinding metal echoed down the corridor, coming from the left, so Kira ran in that direction. After passing by five airlocks along the curving hall, she spotted Major Sandren making furious entries on a touch-panel. "Major!"

He glanced in her direction. "Kira? What are you—"

"Is it Kaen?" she asked.

"Yes, he signed out a ship. The orders are complete nonsense."

Another shudder wracked the station as the ship strained at the end of its gangway.

"Why didn't the clamps release?"

"It's strange." The major shook his head. "Only half of the undocking procedures were followed. He knows better."

"*Kaen* knows better. But if he's not in control…"

"Either way, we need to stop him."

"That's why I'm here, sir. But I'm surprised I beat the security team."

"How *did* you get here so fast?" Sandren asked.

"Ladder."

"Well, others will make their way up here, but it's going to take some explanation about what's going on. Those are questions I don't know how to answer."

"Too much of that going around." Kira assessed what the major had been doing with the airlock door, seeing he was midway through a poorly executed hack of the overrides. "May I, sir?"

"Please." He stepped aside. "I was never much good at this."

"That's why you have a team, sir."

She got to work redoing Sandren's attempt to override the seal. "Almost got it…"

The lock released and the doors began to part—just as another shudder reverberated through the station.

"Suit, now!" Sandren shouted.

On reflex, Kira activated the emergency deployment for the gloves and helmet on her shipsuit. The collar unfurled and a clear dome enveloped her head while gloves formed around her hands.

Kira was sucked through the opening between the airlock's door panels.

She careened straight down the ruined gangway. The smooth walls sped by her, offering nothing to grab. Before she could react, she passed through the splintered end where the ship had ripped away.

For an instant, everything was quiet and still.

Only a dozen meters ahead, the transport vessel was pulling away, its side airlock still open. Kira had no control over her trajectory, but the gangway had sent her on a course straight for the ship's open airlock. She'd have one chance to stick the landing.

One excruciating second passed in the vacuum of space. Time stood still for Kira as she tumbled through the black toward the ship's airlock, her heart pounding in her ears. She held her breath, bracing for the impact.

She clipped the edge of the airlock on her way through the door. Pain radiated from her right shoulder as she cartwheeled to the side. She struck the other side of the chamber and desperately reached for a handhold. Her first grasp came up empty, but she managed to loop her fingers through on the second attempt.

Kira held on for dear life.

Out of the corner of her eye, she saw a black form hurdling toward her.

"Sandren!" she shouted, though she knew he couldn't hear her.

He flew past her and struck the back wall. Kira held out her hand, and he grabbed it on the ricochet, providing just enough leverage to swing toward the wall and grab a handhold.

Sandren pounded on the emergency hatch seal, and the airlock door slammed shut.

The artificial gravity engaged, and Kira was slowly pulled toward the floor.

A gauge on the back wall turned blue, indicating atmosphere had been restored to the chamber.

She pressed the controls on her neck, and the helmet and gloves folded back into her suit. Sandren did the same.

"Holy shite, that was close," she told him.

"That wasn't exactly what I had planned." The major took a deep breath. "I guess we're on our own."

"Still two against one. We can find a sonic blaster and take him out."

"Not unless we find some noise cancelling earbuds. The blast from a handgun like that will echo like crazy in a small ship like this and knock us out, too," Sandren countered.

"Then what do you suggest, sir?"

"We tackle and shackle the old-fashioned way."

"Why am I not surprised you'd say that?"

"It's been too long since I've been in the thick of action."

Kira grinned and released the inner door. "He'll know we're here, but we still have numbers on our side."

"That we do. Lead the way."

— — —

Kaen-Nox glowered at the computer screen. *"How did they make it on board?"* Nox demanded.

"Members of the Guard are quite industrious," Kaen replied. He tried to hide the satisfied smile in his mind.

He'd been afraid that the ship had broken free too quickly, before anyone had a chance to board. The fact that anyone had made it inside the airlock was a near-miracle, but he'd take it.

The question now was whether his rescuers would be able

to subdue him without harming his body. He was certain that Nox would rather die than be captured. Death wasn't on Kaen's itinerary for the day.

"*You should hand yourself over now, if you want to live,*" Kaen told the alien.

"*Whyever would I do that? I've won.*"

"*They'll have the door to the bridge open in a matter of minutes.*"

"*A course has already been set. By the time they override the controls, we'll be among my people.*"

A bang sounded on the door.

Kaen knew they'd never try to bust through the steel. That was an alert for him, if there was any part of himself. His friends were coming.

"*I sense you getting your hopes up,*" Nox said. "*You're only setting yourself up for disappointment.*"

"*Where are you going to meet your people?*"

"*Gaelon.*"

"*Ah, so that's why no one goes to that system.*"

"*One of the reasons.*"

"*And the others?*" Kaen prompted.

"*I'm surprised you don't know already. It's—*"

The door flew open, and he was on the ground before he had a chance to react.

Kaen-Nox struggled against Major Sandren's grasp on his arms while Kira grabbed his ankles.

"*Just need a little more time,*" Nox said. "*How about something to keep them busy?*"

— — —

Kira swiveled her hands to better hold Kaen's writhing

form. "The cuffs, Major?"

"Working on it," Sandren grunted while slipping one of Kaen's hands through the stasis cuffs they'd grabbed from the supply locker outside the airlock.

The first cuff cinched around the colonel's wrist, and Sandren hurriedly jammed the man's hand into the other.

Kira was just about to force his knees up so they could lock his ankles when Kaen's booted feet kicked free of her hands. One foot struck the side of her head, and she tumbled toward the wall. Sudden anger welled in her—disproportionate for the action. Her limbs started to burn.

No, don't transform! You can't now! She willed herself to calm.

The colonel grunted, slamming a fist into Sandren's face.

Blood poured from the major's nose, but he threw his weight against Kaen. "Kira, the cuffs!"

Still fighting back the impulse to shift, Kira dove onto the colonel's legs and forced his knees to bend. The physical aggression was the perfect channel for the raw emotion flooding through her, and the burning started to diminish.

Sandren strained against the writhing colonel, reaching out the tether to loop around his ankles.

Just a little more... With a surge of strength, Kira got Kaen into the necessary position, and the cuffs cinched tight. She dropped the anchor to the deck, locking Kaen in place.

Kira scrambled backward. "All right!"

The major rested on his knees. "You had me worried there. Your eyes were starting to get glowy."

"Yeah, not sure how I avoided transforming. Maybe I'm getting *some* control."

"I hope so."

Kira rose to her feet. "You know, all in all, that actually

went better than I expected."

Sandren wiped the blood from his upper lip. "Easy for you to say."

She looked at the flight controls. "Never mind. I retract my statement."

CHAPTER 11

KIRA GROANED. *WELL, that's just fantastic.*

"What is it?" Sandren asked.

"The ship is on auto-pilot, preparing to make a jump to the nav beacon outside the Elvar Trinary—but the destination is in the Gaelon System," Kira replied, returning her gaze to the navigation screen.

"So?"

"Aside from the part about the unwanted jump, that's a… bad place to go."

Kaen writhed on the floor, jangling his cuffs.

Sandren frowned. "You need to be more specific."

"I don't know what's there, Major," Kira admitted, "but everyone in the Elvar Trinary knows not to enter Gaelon. It's the adjacent system."

"It doesn't matter. We'll cancel the jump and have the ship turned around in no time." He looked over Kira's shoulder at the controls. "Oh."

"Yeah, I was about to get to the part about a nav override triggering a life support failure."

"How in the stars did he rig this so quickly?"

Kira grimaced. "He didn't get to be a colonel for nothing."

"Fok!" Sandren scanned the panel. "Can you undo it?"

"Honestly? I'm not sure, sir. But in the interest in being productive, yes."

"I'll take it. What can I do to help?"

"I don't suppose you have study notes from the nav system programming final exam on hand, do you?"

Sandren shook his head. "Nope."

"Well, then I guess we need to get into the communications system."

"Now *that* I might be able to help with." Sandren leaped over Kaen so he could access the communications console on the side of the room. "I've had to rewire these a time or two in my day. I should at least be able to get a distress call to base."

"If you can manage it, Nia or Kyle might be able to talk us through how to create a back door into the system so we can undo the nav lock—or at least keep us from jumping to subspace. Six minutes until we're in position for the jump."

"I'll see what I can do."

While Sandren got to work, Kira tried to regain control of the ship.

She tended to think of the colonel as being mostly a paper-pusher, but she had to admit that the work on the system had been genius. Tying the life support to navigation was no small feat, especially in such a short time. But, being a rush job, the work was imperfect.

"Sir, I think I may have something," Kira said.

"Good, because I was able to get a distress signal to base, but any kind of text or voice communication is a no-go for now."

"I think we can do a system reset to wipe out the current

destination without permanently disabling the ship like he intended," Kira continued. "Problem is, that means we'll lose life support for that time—but at least it would cancel the jump."

"How long for a reboot?"

"Eleven minutes."

Sandren smiled. "No problem! Plenty of air and temperature regulation won't be a problem for a lot longer than that."

"Yes, sir. That's not my concern. Trouble is if the system doesn't come back on afterward."

"The Guard will have a ship here before that becomes an issue. Besides, we have our suits."

"Yes, sir."

"I sense another 'but'."

Kira nodded. "Whoever the alien was going to meet, my guess is they'll want him back."

"You think they'll come for him?"

Him… or me. "We don't know anything about this enemy, sir."

"You're right, we can't rule out any possibility. But we need the facilities at the base to figure out how to get the alien presence out of him."

Kaen stared up at them. "He said he can't be removed," he stammered.

"Colonel?" Sandren leaned down toward him. "Are you—"

Kaen cried out in agony and spasmed. "He's mine now. You'll all be."

Sandren straightened. "Kira, hold on that system reset. I have another idea."

— — —

Kaen writhed on the ground as Nox regained control.

"Never betray me again or there won't be any of you left," Nox snarled in his mind.

Clearly, the alien still didn't understand the Guard even after spending three years in Kaen's head. A soldier wouldn't be consumed so easily.

Above him, Kira and Sandren were talking urgently. As much as Kaen wanted to listen to their conversation, it was taking every bit of his concentration to maintain his place near the front of his consciousness.

Kira bent down and looked him in the eyes. *"Colonel, are you in there?"* she asked telepathically.

"You can't help me," Nox replied on his behalf.

Kaen shoved him aside. *"I'm here! Don't let him tell you otherwise, Kira."*

Kira smiled. *"You've got it, Colonel. I'll do whatever I can to help. But right now, you need to help me. How do we undo the navigation lock?"*

"Don't you dare try to tell her," Nox threatened privately to Kaen.

"You have no leverage, Nox. There's nothing you can do to this ship that won't kill you, too, or Kira—and I know how important she is to you."

"Sorry, Nox, but I have to side with the colonel on this one. I see you for what you are."

Nox's surprise was palpable. *"You can hear us?"*

"Yeah, the whole telepathic thing." Kira cocked her head. *"Don't understand us bipedal types as well as you thought, huh?"*

"Your abilities won't get me out of him," Nox spat back.

"Maybe not, but guess what? I don't need Kaen to tell me anything. Push him back as much as you want. I can see your recent memories, Nox, and everything I need to know about the

nav system is right there. I know exactly what I need to do."

"You... you can't!" the alien stammered. *"How...?"*

Kira shrugged. *"Maybe modifying me wasn't such a good idea after all."*

— — —

Sandren watched Kira as she bored into the colonel's mind, her gaze as intense as he'd ever witnessed.

He had no idea if she was making any progress, but it was worth a shot—no sense in risking a reset if it wasn't necessary.

"The nav command..." Kira said, her voice strained.

Sandren came to attention. "What do we need to do?"

"Go into the main nav directory and enter the following code." She listed off an alphanumeric string to him.

"One sec." Sandren did as he was instructed. As soon as the final digit was entered, a command window popped up. "There's a prompt for contingent relays. I have no clue what that means." He frowned at the screen.

"Is there a default setting?" Kira asked.

"Yes."

"Okay, select that. Then things will get tricky. You need to do a physical bypass of the life support system using the wiring under the console."

Sandren nodded. "Just don't tell me we have to reverse the polarity."

A smirk curled Kira's lips. "If only that worked as well as it always seems to in movies."

The major dropped to his knees and peeked under the nav console. The metal plate covering the circuitry had already been removed, and it looked like several wires had been spliced together with crude junctures.

"I think I see the problem," he muttered. "Which ones do I change?"

Kira frowned. "I keep getting an image of a blue wire."

Sandren swore under his breath. There were at least four blue-ish wires he could see. "You're going to have to be a lot more specific."

"You know, the blue—"

"Kira!"

She tore her gaze from Kaen's prone form. "I'll have to look at it myself. I can see it, but Nox keeps trying to cloud my perception."

"Nox? Is that the thing that took over the colonel?"

"That's what it calls itself. It's some sort of conscious presence, but I can't tell what kind of physical form it might possess."

"We can deal with that later." Sandren pointed to the hanging wires. "First, what do we do with *that*? Only two minutes before we jump to subspace and it'll be too late for a reset."

"Right." Kira dropped to her back and began sorting through the wires, her brow furrowed.

Sandren sat back on his heels and allowed her to complete the task without interruption. He was fortunate to be surrounded by such talented colleagues, and Kira was truly one of the best. If he had to be stuck with someone on a ship headed into unknown territory, she was at the top of his list for a partner.

After a tense minute and a half, Kira finally dropped her hands to her side and sat up. "Okay, I think that should do it."

"How sure are you?"

She shrugged. "Enough that I'd rather try to power on the system and see if this works than find out why Gaelon is off-limits."

"We're almost out of time, anyway. Proceed."

"Here it goes." Kira took a deep breath and activated the control panel. She half-closed her eyes as though bracing for an explosion.

Sandren took a step back.

The console beeped, and blue lights illuminated across the display.

Kira grinned. "Good news, sir. We're not going to die."

"Have you regained control of the nav system?"

She tapped on the menu and nodded. "It appears everything is responding. Jump is cancelled."

Sandren took a step toward the pilot's chair. "Well done. Let's get back to—"

An alarm sounded, echoing in the compact chamber.

"What *now*?" Sandren's pulse spiked.

Kira's face drained. She began cycling through the ship's systems to identify the issue. "Sir, we're venting atmosphere."

"Where? How?"

On the floor, Kaen chuckled to himself. "Stop trying to override the nav controls and I'll halt the leak."

Kira scoffed. "Have you forgotten about our suits?"

"You might want to look at it more closely," Kaen replied.

Sandren looked down at his suit and was horrified to see a gash running along the side of his torso. *It must have been ripped in our fight earlier, or maybe when I landed,* he realized. So much for having a functional pressure suit.

"You'll die with us," he told Kaen.

"Oh, no. This physical form is convenient, but it is not my only means of being. If you don't want to die, then stop resisting."

"Too late. Course is already set back to the Guard base," Kira replied.

"Is it, now?" Kaen smirked. "Then why haven't we turned around?"

Sandren ran to look over Kira's shoulder at the controls. "The destination is still set to Gaelon."

"I changed it!" Kira re-entered the Guard base and the system reset again. "It keeps overriding it. Why haven't we jumped?"

Fok! Sandren took a steadying breath.

"Oh! The nav console is resetting," Kira realized. "Shite, that means we'll probably jump as soon as it finishes."

"What are our options?"

"We could try the full system reset, but after seeing this, I'm not sure it will work. At a minimum, I imagine we'll lose life support, like we feared."

"Do it."

"But, sir, your suit…"

"I'll get the patch kit. We can't risk a jump to subspace," Sandren said with a tone of finality.

Kira nodded and turned her attention to initiating the reset.

Sandren leaped over Kaen to access the back storage area of the ship. The patch kit was where it should be in a cabinet near the entry airlock. The materials hardly looked like something that would hold up long-term, but it would have to do. He hurriedly placed the adhesive strips along the tear. By the time he was finished, Kira had completed the preparations for the reset.

"Ready?" she asked.

"You're making a mistake," Kaen objected from the deck.

"If you don't want us to do this, then that means it's exactly what we should be doing," Sandren shot back. He nodded to Kira. "Proceed."

"Here it goes." She initiated the restart sequence.

All the mechanical and electrical systems cut out, leaving the cockpit in darkness. The artificial gravity released, and Sandren slowly floated upward. His stomach turned over, but he took calming breaths to settle his senses.

He waited to the count of sixty before concern began to set in. "Why hasn't it come back on?"

"I don't know," Kira replied through the black to Sandren's right.

Great, we're going to be floating out here until we die. That kind of thinking wouldn't solve the situation. "How visible are we out here powered down?"

"Not very." Just the slightest hint of concern edged into Kira's voice. "Do you think the Guard will have sent a rescue ship by now?"

"That's my hope. I did get off the distress call before the shutdown."

"Good, and we haven't altered course."

"All the same, we're a speck in the black. We need to activate the emergency beacon." Sandren shook his head. "Which was probably right below the patch kit. I wasn't thinking."

"We all have a few things on our minds. Don't worry about it," Kira assured him.

Feeling his way through the dark, Sandren worked through the door into the open area surrounding the airlock. He followed his mental map of where he'd just been, feeling in front of him for a latch to the cabinet. There was no way he'd be able to locate and activate a beacon on feel alone, but there was one item he knew exactly how to find if he could just get the cabinet open.

His hand found the handle and pulled. He ran his fingers

along the inside panel of the door, and a cool cylinder met his probing touch.

"Watch your eyes," he warned Kira. With his own eyes closed, he activated the flashlight.

Red light illuminated the cabin, casting an eerie glow in the small space.

Sandren checked below the patch kit, finding nothing. He moved on to the adjacent cabinet.

"Who outfitted this place?" he grumbled aloud.

"I don't think this ship was ever meant to venture out on its own," Kira replied from the adjacent room.

Sandren opened another cabinet, and his light found its mark: an orange box with all manner of emergency markings. "Got it!"

Without hesitation, he activated the beacon.

He carefully propelled himself back toward Kira in the cockpit. "Now we wait."

Kaen scowled below where he was secured to the bottom deck.

"What will we tell everyone about the colonel?" Kira asked.

"I'll think of something. Maybe that he was exposed to a contagion and needs to go into quarantine," Sandren suggested.

"Why not the truth?" Kira asked.

"Maybe. But we don't want mass hysteria with people accusing each other of being subverted just because someone is acting a little off or having a bad day. We'll need to be clear about the extent of the telepathic control."

Kira frowned. "But we don't know that yet."

"My concerns exactly." Sandren sighed. "Like I said, we'll think of something."

They waited in relative silence for another five minutes

until a shudder ran through the ship.

Sandren's heart leaped as he saw the interior of a cargo bay envelop the *Lisbeth II*, complete with the Guard emblem printed on the wall.

"Thank the stars!" Kira relaxed.

"All in a day's work," Sandren said with a grin. He was drawn back to the deck as the artificial gravity of the larger ship took over.

Kira didn't seem to share his enthusiasm. "There's still the concern about the aliens—or whatever they are—coming for him." She glanced at Kaen.

"Orion Station is one of the most defensible locations we have at our disposal. Until we understand the situation, I think it's the best place we can be," Sandren replied.

She nodded.

Sandren took a deep breath as he regained his footing. "All right, Captain. Let's go have a chat with this Nox."

CHAPTER 12

"ANY WORD BACK from the Guard?" President Joris asked Ellen as soon as she stepped into his office.

"No." Ellen closed the door. She wished she had information to bring him, but after her brief conversation with Leon, she'd been unable to raise any of her contacts.

"Shite." Joris sank into his chair. "If Colonel Kaen is subverted, do you think there are others?"

"Maybe. Who's to know?" Ellen walked over to sit across from the president in one of the visitor chairs.

"It's times like this when I wish Elusia had a bigger military presence."

"We're in the Empire now. They have that muscle to bear on our behalf."

"And what good does that do when they won't return our calls?" Joris grumbled.

"I know, sir," Ellen said in a calm, even tone that belied her private concerns. "We could reach out to the High Dynasty council instead."

"No time to jump through those administrative hoops—

Mysar could attack us at any moment. If the Guard isn't responding to this matter, who's to say anyone else in the Empire would come to our aid in time?"

Ellen wished she had an answer. "We have an agreement with them. We need to trust in our new alliance."

The president eyed her. "Do you really believe that?"

She was about to give a vague deflection but stopped herself. "The recent changes in Taran government were made to give individual worlds more autonomy. We can't go running to the authorities on Tararia with every problem."

"Especially if the Guard has subverted members of its own leadership."

"Yes, sir. My concerns, as well."

"So, we need to take matters into our own hands," Joris mused, steepling his fingers.

"We don't have military might, but there is one thing more valuable."

"Information," Joris completed for her.

"Precisely."

"But to gather information of sufficient value, one would need access to places no Elusian in their right mind would dare enter, given the current political environment."

Ellen tilted her head. "Not all of us are Elusian."

Joris dropped his hands to the desktop. "I wasn't suggesting—"

"No, sir, I know you weren't. But I am."

He focused on her. "What are you thinking?"

Ellen leaned back in her chair and crossed her legs. "Well, I was initially sent to Elusia through an organization secretly working on behalf of the Mysaran government. The position afforded me a number of government contacts. One, in particular, remained a... I wouldn't call him quite a friend, but more than a casual work acquaintance."

Joris raised an eyebrow. "A romantic entanglement?"

"No, nothing like that. He was something of a mentor to me." She paused. "We've spoken since I took this new job with you. He expressed an interest in working together again, should the circumstances align."

"That would be impossible so long as Mysar remains outside the Empire."

Ellen nodded. "But perhaps that offers a reason for a visit. The topic of Elusian and Mysaran relations remains a critical subject regardless of the outside political pressures."

"They still want the Elvar Trinary to remain independent. I doubt they'd be receptive to discussion of unification."

"No," Ellen agreed, "but I can tell them what they *do* want to hear."

"Paint yourself as a traitor to me?"

"It would fit with my original mission objective. For all they know, this promotion within the Elusian government was all a ruse to get close while I remained loyal to my origins."

Joris paled. "That's just the scheming talking, right?"

She gave him a reassuring smile. "Sir, when I pledged myself to you, I meant every word. Elusia is my future. I promise."

He didn't look entirely convinced, but he nodded.

"The cover story would make for an ideal entry back into the Mysaran ranks. It would grant me access."

"That it would," Joris mused. He looked her over. "This would be dangerous for you."

"It will, sir, but I owe it to you and Elusia to take the risk."

"I can't ask you to do this."

"I'm volunteering."

He considered her offer. "What would be your strategy?"

"Get in, gather some information, and provide assistance for the Guard to get inside."

"Would they truly infiltrate a foreign nation's capital building?"

Ellen shrugged. "It's an easier sell than infiltrating, say, this building on Elusia. Outsiders are enemies, allies must be treated as friends. You wouldn't walk into a friend's house uninvited."

"But with an enemy, you do whatever is necessary to protect your own interests." Joris nodded, tapping his fingertips together. "So you go in, pave the way, and then…?"

"I get the Guard access to Chancellor Hale."

Joris frowned. "I know that's the end game, but if the plan fails…"

"We'll have the Guard fully engaged by that point. They'd be obligated to come to our aid."

"I hate making plans contingent on so many hypotheticals."

"Isn't that the root of politics, anticipating potential moves and countering future actions three steps ahead?"

Joris smiled. "Three steps would be child's play."

"You're in agreement, then," Ellen replied with a slight smile of her own.

"You're confident in your contact? What would you tell him?"

"That I have a close working relationship with you, which provides access. There are either possibilities to improve diplomatic relations through the official channels, or I can work through backchannels to get the Mysarans what they really want."

"The independence of the entire Elvar Trinary."

"Precisely. And my bet is that they'll use any means

necessary to accomplish that goal."

"Agreed." Joris sighed. "But what if the Guard refuses to move in after you've laid the groundwork?"

"That's the beauty of the plan," Ellen replied with a smile. "If the Mysarans try anything underhanded with me, that would mean that I, an Elusian citizen—a citizen of the Taran Empire—am in danger. The Guard will be obligated to intervene."

"Forcing their hand to act won't win us any favor."

"Easier to beg for forgiveness than ask for permission."

Joris chuckled. "That adage is always irksome on the receiving end."

"At least by the time we have to beg, we'll have something to show for it," Ellen pointed out.

"If all goes well, yes."

Ellen looked the president square in his eyes. "Let me do this, sir. I think it's our best chance to spur action before the Mysarans can mount an offensive against us."

"Make the arrangements," he consented. "But I expect you back here unharmed. I've grown rather fond of your speechwriting."

"Yes, sir. I have many more yet to write." She rose from her chair.

"Good luck." Joris paused. "And if this is meant to be disguised as an official diplomatic engagement, you should take Nico," he suggested.

"I can't in good conscience bring someone else into that level of danger."

"Not into the facility," Joris clarified, "just a ship docked at the main station. Someone through whom to relay information. He can be trusted."

She nodded. "Good idea, sir. I'll speak with him."

"Be careful. I'll see you soon."

Ellen departed with a deferential nod. She stopped by Nico's post at the reception desk on her way out. He was surprised by the request, but in the style of any good assistant, he asked only enough questions to ensure he had the correct information to complete the travel arrangements. After receiving assurance that her transportation would be arranged, Ellen return to her office to have the more difficult conversations.

Her first call was to Leon, her best chance of getting through to anyone with the Guard. She set up an encrypted channel and entered the direct line he gave her, but she got no answer. She tried again.

Finally, the video feed activated. "Ellen, what is it?" he demanded by way of greeting.

"Hello to you, too."

"This isn't a great time." Leon's violet eyes had a hint of red.

"What's wrong?"

"There's a… situation here," her brother replied.

"What—"

"I can't talk about it, Ellen. Tell me why you called so I can get back to my work."

For a moment, she had second thoughts about telling him her plan. She hated to see her younger brother so distressed, and what she was about to say would only make matters worse. But, for the sake of Elusia—and Valta, by extension—she knew what she had to do.

"Leon, I'm going to Mysar," she stated.

He processed the words for a full ten seconds. "You'… What for?"

"If the Guard won't take action, then we have to."

Leon groaned. "The Guard will take care of Hale, Ellen. We're dealing with a more urgent issue right now, but it's next on the list, I promise."

"Good, then I'll be in place when they're ready to move in."

"Ellen, don't be stupid."

"I'm not. You think the Guard—however good they are—can just walk into a secure government facility and take the chancellor without bringing all manner of grief down on themselves?"

He stared back at her. "Yes, that is *exactly* what they do all the time. It is literally their specialty."

"I don't believe it."

"That's not my problem. Stay on Elusia. We'll take care of this."

"Well, I've talked with President Joris. This is how we want to proceed."

"Ellen, don't," Leon cautioned. "The subverted members of the government may have telepathic abilities. They'll know you're lying to them."

"Good thing Kira taught us about mental guards when we were kids then, huh?"

"Maybe those can stand up to a casual gleaning, but if someone really wants information—"

"If it comes to that, then it's already too late."

"Precisely why you shouldn't do this!"

She shook her head. "It's easy for you to be dismissive from your place, removed from the day-to-day life of people over here. Mysar could attack us and we'd be defenseless!"

Leon massaged the bridge of his nose. "Ellen, you're being reactionary and rash. There's more going on here than you know. Let us deal with this the right way."

"I'm going to Mysar," she insisted. "I'll be in touch once

I'm in position."

"No, don't—"

"Pass on my message to whoever it is that makes decisions. We'll fix the system together." She ended the call before he could protest further.

The call could have gone better, but at least she got the message out. She had every confidence Leon would tell the right people to light a fire within the Guard. Hopefully, her next communication would be more productive. With her heart pounding in her ears, she dialed her contact on Mysar.

"Hi, Dominic," she greeted. "Would you still like to work together?"

CHAPTER 13

KIRA HAD NEVER been so relieved to return to Orion Station. While she'd been on her share of dangerous missions over the years, an impromptu spacewalk was at the bottom of her list of ways for how to have a good time.

Soldiers on the rescue ship, the *Vortex*, had detained the colonel on Major Sandren's orders. They'd raised eyebrows when they saw the prisoner in question, but they said nothing and did as they were told just like they were trained to do.

Now back inside the base and heading toward an interview room, Kira could begin reflecting on the day's experiences. Her own transformation. Kaen's alien parasite. Violation of her home. She wished she could take the afternoon to unwind, but duty demanded she remain focused.

Guards escorted the colonel two paces ahead of her, with Major Sandren walking to her left.

The major also seemed shaken by the day's events, though he gave little external indication. Kira had worked with him enough, though, to notice a slight flush to his cheeks and elevated pulse.

Oh, shite. I shouldn't be able to hear his pulse, she realized.

Her own heart pounded in her ears. She still felt so much like herself that it was easy to forget the changes she was undergoing, yet it was too much for her to ignore.

"Sir," she said tentatively, "I don't know if I should stay out here. Maybe I should go back into quarantine. Knowing that Kaen was part of my change—that this was planned—it makes me even more dangerous."

"I understand your concerns, and I share them," Sandren replied. "But you're the only person who's been able to communicate with whatever it is inside Colonel Kaen."

"Isn't that all the *more* reason to be suspicious of me? Maybe me being able to communicate with it is a form of influence itself."

"You overpowered it on the ship," Sandren pointed out.

"Unless that's what it wanted."

Sandren frowned. "Maybe we can't trust what's happening to you, but we won't get anywhere without more information."

"What if it lies and I can't tell the difference?"

"You did fine work today, Captain," Sandren replied after a slight pause. "Trust your gifts and your instincts."

Kira's stomach twisted. "I'm a liability."

"You're also our best shot at getting through this, risks or not."

She nodded. "Yes, sir."

As much as she wanted to protest further, Kira knew he was right. They needed a telepath to get through to the real Kaen within, and she was the only person on base with the skills and clearance to get the job done.

They reached the room that had been set aside for the interview. Filled with a combination of typical interrogation utilities and the necessary setup for a medical evaluation, the room reminded Kira of the places she'd encountered while undercover in the MTech lab on Valta—circumstances she'd rather forget.

Sandren leaned toward her when they entered the room. "Are you okay?" he asked.

She took a deep breath to clear her mind. "Yes, sir."

He gave her one more appraising look. "All right."

The guards stood Kaen with his back against a pole at the center of the room, cuffing his hands behind.

Doctor Elric stepped forward from a monitoring station along the back wall. "Colonel, we're going to run some scans," he stated.

Kaen—or, rather, Nox inside him—sneered at the doctor. "Your tests won't tell you anything. You'll never understand what I am."

"Our science is more advanced than you seem to think," Elric stated, unruffled. He began attaching sensors to the colonel's head and neck.

"We need to find out how he got... possessed, or whatever it is," Sandren said.

"We will, but first I need to see if we can detect whatever is inside him. If there are others, we need a way to identify those cases," Elric replied.

"What will these sensors reveal?"

"Hopefully, some indication of a physical manifestation of the presence." Elric finished adhering the sensors, and then he grabbed a long wand with a sensor array along one edge. He ran the wand from the colonel's head to toes across his front and then repeated the motion along his back.

Kira crossed her arms as she watched from near the entry door. Kaen's smug expression was so unlike his normal self, especially under the circumstances. She couldn't imagine what it must be like for him to be trapped inside his own body while something masqueraded as him.

Elric returned to the monitoring station and activated the sensors. A representation of a colonel's body appeared on the monitor behind him. "Hmm."

Sandren examined the monitor from next to Elric. "Do you see anything?"

"His heartrate and neural activity are elevated, but there isn't any obvious foreign growth in him," the doctor replied.

"I can't believe I was actually hoping there'd be a worm attached to his spinal column," Sandren muttered.

"That would have suggested a more obvious course for treatment," Elric agreed. "As it stands, though, we'll need to run bloodwork to look for microscopic elements."

The major frowned. "How long will that take?"

"At least half an hour to get preliminary results, but I have no idea how deeply we may need to dive. This is clearly something our standard tests don't look for."

Kaen barked a laugh. "Such simple creatures you are."

"I'm certain you aren't as advanced as you'd like us to believe. It's all science," Elric replied. He prepared a syringe. "Hold still," he instructed, gripping the colonel's arm. He drew a vial of blood then stepped back. "I'll begin analyzing this."

"Bring in Leon and his team," Sandren suggested.

The doctor's brow knitted. "Aren't they busy working on a cure for Kira?"

"It might be connected," Sandren said. "We need to explore this angle first."

Kira's heart dropped, but she understood. An unknown alien presence was a security risk for the entire base—and beyond. Her condition was less pressing.

Elric nodded his understanding and departed with the syringe.

Sandren turned to Kira. "Captain, while the analysis is underway, see if you can glean any information about how Nox infected the colonel."

She inclined her head. "I'll do my best, sir."

Kaen eyed Kira with creepy calm as she approached.

"Colonel, I know you're in there," she stated. "We're going to get you back."

"I already told you, it's a futile exercise," Kaen-Nox said.

"See, I don't think so." Kira positioned herself so she could look directly into the colonel's eyes. She could see the difference now, when Kaen was present versus Nox having control. Whenever she spoke with the alien, it was as though a light was missing from within—the ultimate uncanny valley effect with a living, sentient being. She held back a shudder. "You've been found out. You have nothing left to gain from remaining inside him."

Kaen-Nox chuckled. "Oh, don't I? Every time you react, you tell me more about you. Whatever harm you wish to cause him, it won't hurt me."

"But you have nowhere to go," Kira stated. "If you cooperate, you may be able to go free."

The colonel raised an eyebrow. "First, I know better than to think you'd ever let me go. I know all your secrets now. No matter what you may promise me in an attempt to save your friend, I'd never be allowed to leave."

Kira glanced at Sandren, and he nodded.

"That may be so, but that doesn't mean life has to be uncomfortable for you," Kira continued.

Kaen-Nox scoffed. "If I were to vacate this body, you'd make every effort to kill me. I'm far too dangerous for you to keep around."

"But—"

"Oh, Kira, you're making all the wrong assumptions," Kaen-Nox interrupted. "What makes you think I'm even *in* this body?"

"What?" The question caught Kira completely off-guard. "I'm talking to you now. I've felt your presence."

"A presence, yes. But you understand so little of what I am."

Is that even possible? She'd never considered there wasn't an actual being within Kaen. The notion that its physical presence could exist elsewhere and what she was communicating with now was simply a telepathic projection was… terrifying.

"Sir, can I talk to you for a moment?" Kira asked Sandren.

He nodded his consent and stepped into the hallway with her. "What is it, Captain?"

"It's possible he's telling the truth and might not be physically inside Kaen, sir."

Sandren's scowl creased his brow. "How could that be?"

"I can't even hazard a guess. But if there is some way that these beings can gain remote control of a host—"

"They could be in anyone," Sandren surmised.

Kira nodded. "That's my fear, sir."

"But they're not. I mean, we'd know, right?"

"I don't think we can assume anything."

"Shite." Sandren wiped his hands down his face. "But Nox knows, right? You can see his thoughts, just like any other?"

"In theory, yes. But it's *not* anyone else. There's no way of knowing if its thoughts operate the same way. For all I know, it could be able to think a lie and I'd never know any difference." Kira swallowed. "Like I said, maybe it's only making me think I'm directing the conversation just so it can gain complete control over me."

"I don't think that's the case."

"Why, sir?" Kira questioned. "You're acting like everything is normal with me, but something serious happened. I can't be trusted."

The major studied her face. "You were able to glean what it'd done with the ship earlier today."

"That may have been a ruse. Maybe it wanted to get back here to base."

"Then why try to leave?" Sandren questioned. "Why expose itself in the first place? It could have remained hidden and never tried to escape."

Kira shrugged. "Sir, I'm just speculating here. I don't have answers."

"Neither do I," Sandren admitted. "But I have my instincts. And right now, my gut tells me that this alien presence wants to possess you but it can't. I'll be keeping close watch while you see this through."

"I don't want anyone to get hurt because of me," Kira murmured.

"The very fact that you can express that concern assures me that you're still yourself," the major told her. He reached for the door handle. "The truth will reveal itself in time. For now, all we can do is gather as much information as we can. Find out what Nox knows and we'll try to corroborate that information with verifiable facts."

"Yes, sir."

Sandren nodded and opened the door, gesturing Kira through.

"Have a nice little chat about me, did you?" Kaen-Nox asked.

"You're our favorite topic of conversation, don't you know?" Kira returned to her place facing the colonel. "Now, I believe you were about to tell me all about yourself."

"I don't think so," Kaen-Nox replied.

"Like you have any way of stopping me." *Time to put that theory to the test.* She stared into his eyes, preparing to bore into the shared mind to root out what was Kaen and what was the alien.

"It's a valiant effort, Kira, but I'm in control here," Nox said in her mind.

"You're not stronger than me," she replied. *"I'll find out the truth whether you volunteer it or not."*

"Only if I'm here to tell you. Good luck." Nox's presence disappeared.

"What the…?" Kira wondered aloud. She searched Kaen's mind through his eyes, but there was no hint of Nox—or of Kaen within. It was as though everything had shut down and was inaccessible.

"What's going on?" Sandren demanded.

"He's… gone," Kira stammered.

"The alien?"

"Yeah, but not just him. I don't sense Kaen anymore, either."

Sandren rushed forward and waved his hand in front of Kaen's blank face. "Colonel?"

"That won't do anything." Kira shook her head. "He was telling the truth about not really being here."

"That doesn't explain what happened to Kaen."

Kira wet her lips. "Whatever this race is, they clearly have a deep grasp of consciousness. If they can project themselves into someone, there's no reason they can't take someone and bring them elsewhere."

Sandren paled. "But that's—"

"It's all science, sir. Electrical impulses, chemistry. We know some TSS Agents can perform a sort of astral projection. It's not a stretch that these aliens could have similar skills."

The major took a steadying breath. "Okay, the more important question is, how do we get Kaen's consciousness back?"

"By figuring out whatever it is that tethers a consciousness to a specific individual. Nox is paired with Kaen in some way—it wasn't jumping around to anyone it wanted. If it could do that, it never would have allowed itself to be captured."

Sandren crossed his arms. "Assuming this is a two-way corridor, can we lure Kaen back and figure out how to sever the connection?"

"That's what I'm thinking, sir."

"How do you call to someone who can't hear you?"

Kira cocked her head. "You activate the transmitter. If we can find a physical manifestation of that link, we might be able to activate it."

"But Elric didn't find any physical evidence, and you were just saying that Nox doesn't have a corporeal form."

"The scan may not have been looking for the right thing."

Sandren eyed her. "What do you know?"

"I saw a bit of research on Valta that might be applicable here."

"Then go offer what insights you can to the science team. I'll stay with the colonel and alert you if his state changes," Sandren said.

"Yes, sir. We'll try to have you answers as soon as we can." Kira stepped out of the interview room, her mind reeling from the last interaction with Nox. *How do you defeat an enemy you can't see?*

She took a moment to lean against the wall, focusing on her breathing to regain her center.

"Kira! I just heard what's going on." Leon ran toward her from down the hall.

Her heart leaped when she saw him. "I was about to come to see you."

His face darkened. "I have news, too."

"Did Doctor Elric talk to you about Kaen?" she asked.

"Yes, he just stopped by and told me to pause my research into your new nanites so I can focus on analyzing Kaen. I'll never get anything done if we keep shifting objectives!"

She waited for him to take a calming breath before responding. "I know there's a lot going on. Was that your news?"

"No." He groaned. "Promise not to freak out?"

That almost always means it's freak-out-worthy. Kira frowned. "Why would I?"

"Ellen called. She's going to Mysar, to get inside the government."

"She… what?! Of all the impulsive—"

"Oh, I know. When I tried to tell her she was being an idiot, she hung up on me. Real mature, right?"

"She's going to get herself killed!"

"As much as I want to be angry with her, I'm worried." Leon took a shaky breath. "She concocted some insane plan to embed herself with her old contacts so she could help you get in. You grab the chancellor, then get out together."

"That's…" Kira shook her head. "The Mysarans may take it as an act of war. Ellen—a foreign government employee— infiltrating them on its own would be grounds, but if we were to capture the chancellor…"

He nodded. "She wouldn't see reason. The Elusian

president apparently didn't have faith that the Guard would take action without some additional incentive."

"Like they know anything about our capabilities." Kira rubbed her eyes. "Shite, I really didn't need anything else to worry about."

"It's not your job to get her out of this mess."

"Except it kinda is."

Leon looked her over with concern. "Kira, are you okay?"

"Yeah, I'm fine." It was a lie, and he knew it.

Leon enveloped her in his arms, and she happily buried her face in his chest. "You're who I'm worried about the most," he murmured into her hair. "You should be relaxing, not out—"

Kira pulled out of the hug and held him at arm's length. "This is what I do, remember? I know what I can take. I'm okay."

Reluctantly, he nodded. "I'll get used to it eventually, though I don't have to like it."

She gave him a quick kiss. "Thank you for your concern, but we have work to do."

"Right, the alien."

"The colonel is in far more immediate danger than me. That's priority."

"You're *my* priority."

Kira looked him in the eyes. "Leon, you're working for the Guard now. This is about what's best for the Empire, not us personally."

After a moment, he nodded and released a slow breath. "I'll get back to figuring out what's going on with you as soon as I can."

She took his hand and squeezed it. "I know you will. But don't let me be a distraction. Whatever has taken control of Kaen is likely the same type of entity that's controlling Hale.

Figure out what's going on with him, and maybe we'll have a solution for how to help her, too."

"Okay."

"Now, I may have some information that didn't seem relevant before," Kira continued. "Let me tell Sandren about Ellen, and then why don't you show me this lab of yours?"

CHAPTER 14

"I DON'T GET it," Leon muttered half to himself. He pushed back from the workstation in his lab and crossed his arms.

Next to him, Kira had been watching him perform the analysis of Kaen's scans. "So, you don't see anything amiss?"

"No," Leon replied. "There don't appear to be sufficient neurological variations to account for Kaen's present condition."

"It would seem telepathy doesn't take up much neural real estate," Jack added.

"But this is about a whole consciousness, right? Not just telepathy," Leon said.

Jack extended his hand in the air, palm open. "What *is* consciousness?"

Leon scowled at him. "You're not helping."

"Settle down, boys," Tess interjected from her cluttered workstation on the opposite wall. "There are a lot of unknowns here. We need to be systematic."

"Griping about the monumental task is all part of the process." Leon smirked.

"Yeah, yeah." She chuckled and crossed her arms. "But seriously, what gives? I'd expect there to be all sorts of weirdness going on inside him."

Jack let out a long breath. "It's not *that* surprising. After all, it went unnoticed for three years."

"He was altering his own medical records," Leon pointed out. "The changes were subtle, but there was a definite shift in neurochemistry."

"True," Tess conceded, "but beyond that, who's to say that there needs to be anything physically different to enable control? Kira's just like the rest of us, right?"

Leon nodded. "That's true. They've never found a medical reason for Valtan telepaths to—"

"Actually, that's not quite true," Kira cut him off. "I didn't want to bias your assessment before, but Jared revealed something about telepathic abilities back at the MTech lab."

"And you've been sitting on that information?" Leon questioned with a raised eyebrow.

"It may be nothing, so I wanted to see if you had other leads." Kira leaned her arms on the high table in the center of the room. "MTech was using some sort of new imaging technique—maybe something from that recent Aesir technology disclosure. He and Monica had found a part of my brain that seemed to resonate with the telepathic output or something."

Leon perked up. "Do you remember where that was?"

"More or less." Kira approached his workstation and examined the monitor. "Here, I think." She traced her finger between the left inferior frontal gyrus and the supramarginal gyrus.

"That's right in the speech and sensory centers," Leon assessed. "It'd make sense."

"Huh. Well look at that," Tess said. "I can't believe we all missed that." She pointed to a slight dark spot in Kaen's neural scan, which branched between the two areas Kira had identified. The line was no more than a hair's width, and they'd dismissed it as a defect in the scan.

"Yeah, that's it," Kira confirmed. "It was most distinct in Jared's scan, probably thanks to their imaging tech."

"Could that tiny structure really be responsible for such complete telepathic control?" Leon mused aloud.

"Well, there's nothing else out of the ordinary here," Jack replied. "If that's the only thing different, then it must mean something."

"Hmm." Leon's eyes met Kira's. "Maybe it's time we talk with Jared."

She nodded. "I was just thinking the same thing."

"How soon can that be set up?" he asked her.

"Probably right away. I think Sandren has been looking for a verbal punching bag."

"Do you think I could sit in and try to get his input on this analysis?" questioned Leon.

"I'll ask," Kira replied and slipped from the room.

Jack watched her go. "She seems to be taking everything in stride."

"She's always had a knack for that." *I'd be losing it if I had an unknown alien presence inside of me.* Leon sighed. *And here I am one of the few people who could maybe help her, and I have no idea where to start.*

Regardless of how helpless he felt at present, he had a job to do. Kira and Kaen were both counting on him to find a solution.

"All right," Leon said to his team, turning back to the business at hand. "That neural connection is a physical thing.

What's it made out of?"

"The closest substance in our database is ateron, but it's not that. The density analysis looks suspiciously like the nanite sample Kira brought back from MTech, but we'd need to take a sample to be sure," Tess said.

"Except that Jared saw a neural structure in her scan *before* she was infected with the Robus nanites," Leon countered.

"And nanites usually don't clump together like this," Tess pointed out.

Leon nodded. "Everything on Valta and in MTech's research deviates from what we've seen elsewhere." He looked at his team. "What if the Valtan telepaths were *made*?"

Tess placed her hand on her chin in an exaggerated thinking pose. "How could we have missed nanites in the Valtan population?"

"Yeah, that would come up in medical exams, right?" Jack added.

"It's possible that records have been doctored over the years—Kaen certainly managed that within the Guard." Leon shifted in his chair. "I mean, it's too big of a coincidence that Kira would have something identical to Kaen. All of this tech originated in the same system."

"Holy shite," Tess whispered.

Jack's eyes bugged out. "Is that possible? That the telepaths on Valta are all controlled by the same aliens?"

Leon groaned. "No! That's not what I'm suggesting at all. I'm wondering if maybe the aliens are from Valta or inhabited it at some point. Maybe they left something behind on the planet that affects certain people."

"Right, yeah." Tess flushed slightly.

"But Kaen isn't Valtan," Jack interjected. "How would he have been exposed?"

"I don't know," Leon admitted. "But if we're right about this neural structure being made out of nanites, we can develop a test to see who might be under telepathic influence."

Tess stared at him solemnly. "But if that structure is some kind of receiver, doesn't that mean Kira is susceptible to control herself? And you?"

Leon hadn't wanted to consider that possibility, but he couldn't ignore the potential. "We can't rule anything out. But we do know that Kira has faced off against the alien presence and not been subverted. Maybe being a telepath herself changes the dynamic. As for me... I'm Valtan, but I'm definitely not telepathic, as Kira would be quick to tell you. So, I don't know. I'll need to be tested like anyone else."

Jack nodded. "Okay, one step at a time. First, we're looking for evidence of these neural structures in people who aren't Valtan. Should be easy to cross-reference with old medical exams."

A message popped up on Leon's workstation. It was from Kira: >>Sandren agrees we should interview Jared and see what he knows. We could use your expertise to ask the right questions about the neuroscience.<<

>>I'm in,<< Leon wrote back. >>Where should I meet you?<<

Kira sent a map to him, detailing the destination and an optimized route.

Leon looked up at his team. "We got the go ahead to talk with Jared. Can you two try to work out an automated way to check for that telepathic structure?"

"Sure," Tess agreed, "but we really need to give it a name."

Jack nodded. "We do. I already can't stand 'the structure' as a nickname, and I've only been using it for five minutes."

"What about 'telepathic receptor', or TR for short?" Leon suggested.

Tess and Jack looked at each other and shrugged.

"Works for me," Tess said.

Leon smiled. "It's got a name, so now you can define it."

— — —

Kira glared at Jared across the interview table. He was being entirely too calm for the situation. *He should be afraid right now. What happened to the twitchy man from Valta?*

Behind her, Sandren shifted as he leaned against the wall next to Leon. "You may as well talk, Jared," the major urged. "You know what Kira can do to you."

"Do your worst," the scientist replied.

Kira could sense Leon's concern. Even though they'd grown up together, he had never witnessed the darker side of her abilities up close. Part of her didn't want him to see that side of her, but if they had any chance at a future together, she needed to bare her full self—whatever that self was now.

Ignoring those around her, Kira spread her hands on the tabletop and stared into Jared's eyes. "Tell me what you know about the Valtans' telepathic abilities."

"There's not much to tell," he replied.

"We saw an artificial neural bridge between the left inferior frontal gyrus and the supramarginal gyrus," Leon interjected. "What do you know about the expression of telepathic abilities in that region?"

"We saw it in a number of Valtan creatures but never on other worlds," Jared explained.

Kira glared at him. "Is that how the aliens were controlling Monica?"

The scientist laughed. "Monica? She was never under telepathic control."

"So, she was a willing participant?" Kira prompted.

"Most of us were. It was important work. We were the ones willing to do what no one else would."

Kira shook her head. "That kind of thinking has always led Tarans down a dark path. You're just as bad as the Priesthood was."

Sandren stepped forward. "Some collaborators were willing participants, but these aliens have taken over others against their will. Who are they? What are they after?"

Jared stiffened in his chair. "I only know about our work."

"You're not telling us everything." Kira stared into his eyes.

"I've said all I care to share."

"You know I don't need your permission," she cautioned.

He glared back at her.

"Suit yourself." Kira bored inside, peeling back the layers of his consciousness that so thinly veiled his inner mind.

The information she sought was there for the taking, if she could locate it. A lifetime of memories and knowledge spread out before her. Random connections led to tangents of the mind, with the timeline of experience having no bearing on how the history was organized. She would have to dig, and the more Jared resisted, the more it would hurt him.

He cried out in pain as she began the process. She was vaguely aware of Sandren's and Leon's discomfort in the distance, but that wasn't her concern. This was her job, and she was good at it.

Minutes passed as Kira dug through the disjointed archive of Jared's experience, seeking the time when he was at MTech's lab on Valta. He had to have seen something, talking about something with Monica, which would offer insight into their present predicament.

In time, she found an impression of Valta and traced the

thread back to a bundle of memories. Flashes of Monica came to the surface, of working with her in the MTech lab and committing their atrocious experiments on innocent people. Jared had been a willing participant in it all.

"Jared didn't come to Valta until later," Kira said aloud to the observers. "I don't think he arrived much before me."

"He seemed to know an awful lot for being a latecomer," Leon said.

"Yes, he was definitely involved in some way before," Kira agreed. "I'll have to do some more digging to find out where."

She returned to her prodding, searching for another thread that would lead her to earlier in Jared's career, when he had first been corrupted. He had been a willing participant with the aliens—she could feel it. When she'd probed Kaen's mind earlier, she felt the strife of his situation. Here, though, Jared was all-in.

He had handed himself over to control years ago, even if he wasn't an active host. She should have sensed that when she controlled him briefly while back on Valta, but it wasn't something she had been looking for. Now, though, understanding the context, she was struck with a pang of pity for how misguided he'd been.

Kira tugged on the various threads leading from Jared's time on Valta, searching for the one that would yield the answers she sought. Eventually, one caught her attention: a connection straight to MTech's headquarters on Mysar.

She separated her mind from his just enough to relay the information to the observers. "He worked for MTech at their headquarters. Someone in the senior leadership brought him in—a man. They told Jared he had a special part to play."

Kira watched the memories play in her mind's eye as she lived through Jared's eyes. His recollection was hazy, and she struggled to make sense of the images and feelings passing through her.

"A man gave him an injection," she continued. "Jared couldn't see it, but he felt it. That must be how they transfer the nanites."

"Like when Monica stuck you with that syringe?" Leon asked from behind.

Kira relived the memory again. "I think so. The strange man handled it like a precious commodity. I don't get the impression that it's something they give to just anyone."

"That limits the number of potential hosts," Sandren assessed. "Good for us."

"Yes," Kira concurred, "but this also means we have a bigger issue on our hands. Monica didn't just go rogue on Valta—MTech's leadership is involved."

"I wonder…" Leon mused. "I saw a man with the Mysaran chancellor on Valta. What are the chances it's the same man you just saw in this memory?"

Kira shook her head without breaking eye contact with Jared. "Pretty high, and I bet you he's an MTech exec."

Sandren groaned. "So, MTech and the Mysaran government are both compromised. What a foking mess."

"Fortunately, the Guard just happens to specialize in fixing that sort of situation," Kira said with a slight smile.

"Let's not get ahead of ourselves," the major cautioned. "We know how they get the nanites in, but how do we get them out?"

Kira combed through more memories, seeking any indication of a weakness. *Tell me,* she demanded of Jared, echoing the thought throughout his mind.

"They're always so hungry," he replied at last. *"They feed on the darkness within us."*

She almost dismissed the thought at first, thinking it too ridiculous, but she sensed truth in his statement. *They thrive on suffering,* she realized. No wonder Monica had made such a perfect ally.

"Then how do you drive them out?" Kira pressed.

"You must starve them," he replied. *"Change the neural chemistry. So long as there is stress and loneliness, they can survive. In a serene mind, they can be driven out."*

Something stirred underneath Jared's consciousness, just out of reach. It snarled at Jared as he revealed the secrets that were never supposed to be shared.

Kira's heart jumped into her throat as she felt Nox's presence. "Shite, it's here!"

"What?" Sandren demanded.

"Nox," Kira explained. "I can feel it."

"How did it get out of Kaen?" Sandren questioned.

Kira began to connect the pieces in her head. "If it never was *physically* in Kaen, it can jump bodies… but maybe only to an extent."

"My team is developing a test for the neural markers that indicate the telepathic receptor—or TR, as we've dubbed it for now," Leon cut in. "Jared will make the perfect test case."

Sandren took a step toward the door. "Then there's no time to waste. Let's get him to your lab."

"I suggest we bring Kaen, too, sir," Kira said. "If we started to drive Nox out, it may start jumping between potential hosts."

"What if there are other hosts?" Sandren asked.

"It's unlikely there are others in this base," Kira countered. "If I were an alien looking to gain leverage, Jared—a captive—is the last person I'd jump into. When it left Kaen, I'd wager it only went to Jared because it had no better option. Its ability to take control has to have something to do with that TR Leon's team identified."

The major nodded. "I'll agree with that logic."

"And this is going to sound weird, but the key to beating these guys is to be… happy," Kira said tentatively.

Sandren eyed her. "Please explain, Captain."

"The nanite structure that they build requires a certain neural chemistry to remain intact. It's the kind of chemical cocktail that comes from emotions on the negative side of the spectrum. If you're happy, the chemistry shifts." She glanced at Leon. "This would explain why they could never get ahold of me. Despite all the craziness going on, I have the new—or, renewed—relationship bliss thing going on."

"Then why do you still have telepathic abilities?" Sandren asked.

"Well, just because this TR appears in the same place, that doesn't mean the mode of creation is the same," Leon replied. "There's still some mysterious 'X factor' with Valta. Whatever alien nanotech is in Kaen and Jared right now likely isn't identical to what enables abilities in Valta's Readers."

"Yeah, no one is going around sticking mopey Valtan kids with syringes full of nanites, I'm sure of that," Kira added. "Whatever causes those abilities is a more natural means." She looked over at Jared. "He doesn't know, but Nox does."

"I don't think our alien friend is in a sharing mood," Sandren said.

Kira stared into Jared's eyes. *"What do your people want with me, Nox? What makes Valtans so special?"*

The alien didn't reply.

"Tell me, Nox!" Kira demanded. *"Are you from Valta?"*

The alien resisted, but she cut into the entity's mind until she found the answer she sought. There were more of the beings, but not in a sense of life Kira understood.

She felt the alien's memories—shared across the consciousness of many. They had been one with the network of life on Valta long ago. It had allowed them to expand their consciousness in a way they'd never dreamed. But the process left something behind. Even after they left Valta, their remnants remained, and those had changed the people on Valta. Those remnants were the source of Kira's telepathic gifts.

Her heart caught in her throat. *"Where did you go? Back home?"* She was desperate to know more, to understand how she came to be.

Nox ignored her pleas, but her determination drove her deeper into its mind. Eventually, she saw an image of a vast, empty space.

"Valta was not the first, and it was never meant to be the last," Nox finally admitted. *"When Tarans came along, we saw a new opportunity to venture as autonomous beings. They were our chance to once again be among the stars. They took us to a new system where we could grow."*

Kira shook her head. *"Gaelon. And you told your hosts to spread the word for no one to ever go there, so you could multiply undisturbed."*

Nox tried to hide its thoughts from her, but Kira could sense the affirmation.

"Why?" she pressed, focusing her telepathic might. *"What did you need from Mysar and Valta?"*

The alien's resolve buckled, and it submitted it. *"We sought a new vessel to carry us so that we could exist beyond this physical plane, even as we move through it in an isolated body. And soon, we will have the template for that new vessel."*

That's what they want me for, Kira realized and broke the

telepathic link. She relayed what she'd seen.

"That explains it!" Leon exclaimed. "Kira, I think you're immune."

"Why?"

He stroked his chin. "Think about it, the aliens can exert control over great distances, but you require eye contact to initiate a Reading. The TR connects the right neural pathways to enable telepathy, but it's like an offline version of it."

"What about Kaen's influence over others here?" Sandren asked.

"My guess is that the alien could exert close-range telepathic control through direct eye contact, like Kira. But beyond that, it's limited to a host with a suitable TR—something formed through whatever augmentation Jared and Kaen were given," Leon replied.

Kira nodded. "That seems to be the case."

"Got it," Sandren said. "But, how does that impact Kira's susceptibility for control?"

"To extend the analogy," Leon replied, "she has an incompatible receiver. To put it bluntly, if the nanites Monica gave you, Kira, were capable of modifying your existing TR to function as a receiver, then I'd expect Nox to be in your mind right now and not Jared or Kaen."

"True," Kira agreed. "So, I guess we need to get everyone in a good mood until we confirm that no one else has a TR."

Sandren chuckled. "Great, so the solution to all our problems is to play love ballads over the station's loudspeakers."

"Yeah, pretty sure that would horribly backfire."

"But in all seriousness," Leon interjected "if this is a matter of neurochemistry, that's an easy fix. We can try a few neural cocktails and see if the TR in Kaen dissolves."

"That sounds like a genuine plan." Kira cracked a smile.

"That it does," Sandren agreed. "Let's save the colonel."

CHAPTER 15

KAEN'S SENSE OF self was just out of his grasp. Before, when Nox had taken control, Kaen had remained aware of his surroundings, his body, his individual thoughts. Now, he was adrift.

He had no idea how much time had passed in his bizarre state of nothingness, or if he was within himself or outside. As much as he searched for a sense of direction, there was nothing to see.

So, he waited, as patiently as he could, for a sign.

I'm still me, he tried to reassure himself. *I wouldn't be thinking these thoughts if I weren't. But where am I?*

The waiting was torture, but he had no choice.

Finally, after what felt like an eternity, the darkness began to clear.

Kaen strained to orient himself in his surroundings, as though looking through a thick fog. Sights and sounds were distorted, but he was able to make out enough to determine he was somewhere within the Orion Station base.

Good, I'm among friends. Relief flooded through him,

startling him with the sensation. *I can feel again!*

It was a very promising sign, indeed.

Too much was still indistinct for him to draw conclusions about his present circumstances, so he continued to wait in the fading blackness.

Then, a warm presence brushed up against his thoughts. *"Colonel, are you there?"*

Kira. Kaen could feel her. *"Yes, I'm here!"* he replied.

"Nox jumped into Jared," Kira explained. *"I was able to find out some more about how the aliens maintain control. They manipulate your neurochemistry. We're trying to counter the effects now."*

"Tell me what you need me to do."

Kira chuckled in his mind. *"This is going to sound ridiculous, sir, but I need you to think happy thoughts."*

"Pardon?" the colonel replied in a skeptical mental tone.

"The aliens thrive on negative energy. We're giving you a healthy dose of the happy brain drugs right now, but you'll need to help the process along."

"I never would have guessed that." Kaen soaked in the information. *"How did you figure that out?"*

"We were able to get some information from Jared. Turns out his bad attitude was by design."

"Come to think of it, Nox's power over me waned whenever I held a strong sense of hope."

"Love, hope, it all undermines their strength."

Kaen laughed in his mind. *"I knew being in love with my work would pay off."*

"That's the spirit, Colonel. I'll be right back. We're going to up the dose."

Kira vanished from his mind.

A moment later, Kaen was hit with a rush of energy. His

fingers and toes tingled, the sensation creeping up his arms until it enveloped his core. He breathed in a deep breath, filling the lungs he could once again feel and control of his own accord.

The cloud lifted from his vision. Kira stood next to the medical bed on which he was reclined. Leon and Doctor Elric were engaged in a frenetic discussion at a nearby computer terminal. At the foot of the bed, Major Sandren looked on with a concerned expression that was just beginning to turn toward one of relief.

Kira leaned forward and stared into Kaen's eyes. Her mental presence cut through the intense rush from the drugs. *"It's working, Colonel. You're doing great."*

Kaen thought back to his career in the Guard, surrounded by the friends who were his family. No matter what adversity he faced, they were always there to help each other.

Kira fed into his thoughts, willing him to continue.

"That's it!" Leon said from across the room. "It's breaking apart."

Sudden pain radiated through Kaen. "Argh!"

"What's happening?" Kira questioned.

"It looks fine on screen," Doctor Elric replied, "but his blood pressure just shot up."

"You're okay, Colonel," Kira tried to soothe. *"Keep thinking those happy thoughts."*

"You think positive thinking is enough to stop me?" Nox sneered.

Kaen recoiled. *"No, stay away!"*

The alien mind wasn't inside Kaen this time, he realized. It was only a visitor at the edge of his consciousness, much like Kira.

"You're finished, Nox," Kira jeered back. *"We know your weakness now."*

"This conflict hasn't even begun."

Just as suddenly as it had arrived, Nox vanished.

"Blood pressure is normalizing," Doctor Elric reported.

Leon smiled. "The TR is no longer showing up on active scan."

Kaen took a slow, steady breath. The oppressive weight that had been bearing down on him for days was gone. "Well, that was something." He chuckled. "I never thought I'd be so excited to talk again."

Kira beamed. "It's good to have you back, sir."

Kaen cautiously sat up on the medical bed. "I hope it goes without saying, but I apologize for anything I may have said or done while under Nox's influence."

"Of course, sir. Think nothing of it," Sandren acknowledged with a nod.

"Much of it's a blur, but what I do remember isn't particularly friendly," Kaen continued. "Nice work stopping that transport ship before anyone was seriously injured."

Sandren cracked a smile. "Most action I've seen in years. Kira was who saved the day."

"Did you learn anything else about where Nox was trying to take you, or what it was after?" Kira asked, always one to focus on the mission at hand.

"He activated me so I could watch over you," Kaen replied frankly. There was no sense in skirting the issue.

Kira looked down. "I figured as much."

"He kept referring to you as a 'template' for whatever his people are planning. I don't know who or what they are, exactly, but Gaelon is their stronghold."

Kira exchanged glances with the others in the room. "We know. And as concerning as that is, we have a more pressing issue. It's come to our attention that the Mysaran chancellor has been compromised."

Memories of the deleted communications flooded back to Kaen. "I wanted to tell you so badly, but…"

"Nox was very strong, sir. I barely got the upper hand, and I've been training in mental combat for most of my life. It wasn't you doing those things," Kira soothed.

Kaen knew she was trying to help, but the words offered no comfort. He'd allowed himself to become a liability to the organization he'd sworn to protect. Time and a renewed commitment to service were the only way to make peace with what had happened.

He swung his legs over the edge of the bed and hopped down. "Elric, I need to be cleared for duty. Is there any reason to suspect I am still subverted?"

The doctor looked to Kira.

"I detected no lingering presence in him," she replied, "but we don't know if it could come back."

"The TR is completely dissolved," Leon added, "but, likewise, it might not stay gone."

Doctor Elric nodded with consideration as he listened to their advice. "In my professional opinion, Colonel, you are presently not under alien influence. However, I must request that you come in for a scan twice per day until we can determine if there's a chance for reemergence. This might not be over yet."

"Agreed," Kaen stated.

"Otherwise, I see no reason to hold you here between those check-ins, especially given the unique insights you can offer about the enemy," Elric concluded.

"Thank you." Kaen turned to Sandren. "I need to brief the leadership. Tell me everything you know about the situation with the chancellor."

— — —

Kira felt drained after her venture inside Kaen's mind, but there was no time to rest.

At Kaen's insistence, the group immediately adjourned from the lab to a conference room so they could discuss potential next steps for the colonel to present to Guard command. As they walked toward the meeting space, Kira took the brief opportunity to process the recent events.

She didn't want to let on to the others just how far gone Kaen was when she'd finally been able to make contact. Whatever Nox did, it was only Kaen's sheer willpower and dedication to his position that had kept him from being forever lost within himself. A weaker individual might not have been so fortunate.

Facing that kind of power to manipulate matters of the mind was a new challenge for her. Even though she'd spent the majority of her life as a telepath, tasks involving those skills had always come easily to her. Never before had she faced a foe she couldn't read or control. It scared her.

In a position where she had historically lacked physical might compared to her comrades, she'd always had that one advantage. Now, her physical capabilities were a major wildcard and she was up against telepaths more powerful than herself.

Figures this would happen right when I have the most to lose. Her thoughts drifted to her team and the fulfilling life she'd built in the Guard, and how having Leon with her now offered a chance to make it even more. The future might be uncertain, but she had a lot to fight for. And she wouldn't give up.

"What do you think, Kira?" Kaen asked.

Oh, shite, was I supposed to be listening? Kira quickly returned to the present. "I'm sorry, sir, I—"

The colonel cracked a wan smile. "Quite all right, Captain. I think we're all a little distracted after what we've just been through."

"All the same, sir, I should have been paying attention. What was your question?"

"More of a comment," Kaen continued. "This alien presence is too significant a threat to be ignored. Though Mysar isn't in the Empire and shouldn't otherwise be our problem, to leave the Mysaran leadership unchecked may introduce future complications for us."

"I agree, sir," Kira said, honored that Kaen acknowledged she could make a contribution when it came to the unusual nature of this enemy.

"A plan is already in the works," Sandren chimed in. "Leon's sister, Ellen, who now works as the press secretary for the Elusian president, took it upon herself to travel to Mysar."

"This is the same woman you called when we were on Valta, correct?" Kaen clarified.

Leon nodded. "Yes, sir. She has a frustrating tendency to take matters into her own hands."

"I'm getting that impression." The colonel frowned. "If we send in a team to apprehend the chancellor, Ellen might be a liability."

"But she could also be an asset," Sandren advised. "Having someone on the inside could facilitate us gaining entry to the capital without causing a scene. We have no idea how many people may be subverted within the government. An outsider is really the only person we can be sure is clean."

They reached the conference room, and the members of the party spread around the table. Sandren activated the desktop to bring up the notes he and others had gathered in regard to the developing situation.

Kira took a seat next to Leon and scanned over the summary. She noticed a file related to the chairman of MTech.

"That's him," Leon said, pointing to the thumbnail portrait of the chairman. "That's the man we saw with the chancellor in the MTech lobby on Valta."

"Who else knows about this?" Kaen questioned.

"The rest of Kira's team was with him," Sandren replied. "I haven't officially filed a mission report—given everything that's happened—so aside from them, just the people in this room know."

"Let's keep it that way," Kaen instructed. "If word gets out there are aliens capable of taking over someone's mind, we could face a situation of mass hysteria. Further, we don't need to bring down a political shitestorm on ourselves about all the reasons we shouldn't get involved in Mysar's affairs. We need to take care of this before it becomes a bigger issue, end of story."

"We're with you, sir." Sandren nodded.

The colonel folded his hands on the tabletop. "Good. I know your trust in me must be shaken after how I was taken over by Nox, but I intend to earn back that trust."

"It could have happened to anyone, sir," Kira said. "I'll be the first to let the proper authorities know if I detect anything out of place."

"Thank you, Captain. And I'll be sure to check in with Doctor Elric and Leon regularly to monitor for any signs of resurgence. Telepathic assessments won't be possible while you're on Mysar."

"Sir?" Kira's brow knitted.

"We don't know how many aliens there might be, or what

their endgame is. We have surmised that the Robus were intended to be new hosts for them, and you, Kira, were supposed to be a prototype to present to a… benefactor of some sort. This is bigger than just the Mysaran government, but we do know that Chancellor Hale is an important piece of the puzzle. I want you to retrieve her and do for her what you've done for me."

"Could you maybe prepare a serum for the chancellor that could be used in the field to dissolve the TR?" Sandren asked Leon. "That would mitigate some risks."

Leon frowned. "I wish we could, but the neurochemistry levels need to be monitored too closely for us to guess at dosing. Outside of laboratory conditions, a serum might do more harm than good."

"So we need to bring her back here," Kira concluded.

Sandren sighed. "An extraction, it is."

"Sir, if I may…" Kira waited for Kaen's nod of approval. "We don't know when Hale was subverted. The chancellor's persona might actually be the alien influence."

"That occurred to me, as well," the colonel replied. "If that's the case, then the Mysarans will be given the opportunity to select a new leader."

"Yes, sir," Kira acknowledged. "As much as I want to help set things right on Mysar, I don't know if it's a good idea for me to be out in the field. What if I were to lose control and change?"

Kaen nodded. "Were the circumstances any different, I'd evaluate other options. However, you're the only person in the Guard who we know can stand up to the aliens' telepathic influence. You may be a wildcard, but you're also mission-critical."

Kira took a slow breath. "Yes, sir. I'll do my best."

The colonel swept his hand across the desktop to clear the workspace. "Now, we have an infiltration to plan."

CHAPTER 16

SOME MISSION PLANNING sessions left Kira energized to get into the field. The latest meeting had quite the opposite effect.

As soon as they were dismissed, Kira beckoned for Sandren to hang back. "Sir, may we have a frank discussion about this plan?" she asked.

"All right." He motioned her back into the conference room and closed the door. "What's on your mind?"

"This mission has no chance of going according to plan. The assumptions we're making about the Mysaran government building are most likely wrong, we have a single 'in' who may or may not be able to offer any leverage or insights, and I barely have any confidence in my own ability to keep it together."

"You've never been one to question your abilities, Kira."

She stared at him wide-eyed. "That was before they turned me into a foking Robus!"

"Fine, you want a frank discussion?" Sandren crossed his arms. "I *don't* think you should be out in the field. My responsibility is to keep all my soldiers safe. Having you out there with Kyle, Nia, and Ari puts them at greater risk. But Kaen was right about you being mission-critical. We're dealing with a group of telepathic entities, and you're the only person who's proven herself capable of assessing that threat in a meaningful way."

"Gah!" Kira paced in a small circle. "I hate not being able to trust myself!"

"Look, you're agitated now and are still in control. You need to have faith you'll maintain that lucidness when it matters."

She checked herself, realizing that letting her emotions get the better of her only made a slip more likely. "I'll be with my team. If anyone can keep me grounded, it's them." *Though I wish Leon were coming along, too.*

"Once we have Hale in hand, we can figure out how deeply this alien conspiracy runs. Hopefully by then, Leon will also have identified treatment options for you."

"Yes, sir."

"But, Captain, I can't take your ability to maintain control on blind faith. I'm going to have Doctor Elric prepare a sedative for your team to have on hand, just in case."

"And that will work through metallic scales?"

"He's assured me that it's a very effective delivery mechanism."

She nodded. "All right, that makes me feel better."

"I'm sure it won't come to that."

"Always be prepared," she reiterated.

"Right. Now, was there anything else?"

Kira shook her head. "No, I said what I needed to say for my own peace of mind. Thank you, sir."

"Okay. Let's go brief the rest of the team."

The challenging circumstances still weighed on Kira's

mind, but knowing there was a contingency plan to make sure her team would be safe assuaged her biggest fears. Now, her foremost concern was if she'd be able to stand up to the entity that had overtaken Hale.

Kira and Sandren walked to the shared residence of her teammates, and she knocked on the door when they arrived.

Kyle answered. "Major. Kira! You're out of quarantine."

The others jumped from their bunks.

"How are you feeling?" Nia asked.

"I'm good," Kira replied. "May we come in?"

"Of course." Kyle stepped aside.

Kira entered and sat down at the table, while Sandren remained standing by the door.

"Kira's condition is still uncertain," Sandren stated. "However, the circumstances demand her involvement in a more serious matter. We were able to successfully remove the alien presence from Colonel Kaen, as far as we know, but the information we learned about the aliens points to a conspiracy throughout the Mysaran government. We need to apprehend Chancellor Hale."

"Are we going to Mysar?" Ari asked.

Kira nodded. "We've planned a covert infiltration of the government building. Ellen—Leon's sister—has gone ahead to establish herself with the government, and she should be able to help get us in."

Kyle half-raised his hand. "Does that entire family have some sort of fixation with being informants for the Guard?"

Kira snorted. "They're a meddlesome bunch. Even with her assistance, we'll need our stealth gear and your hacking wizardry to get the access we need."

"That's what we do best," Nia said with a smile. "Is it just the four of us?"

"Yes, core team," Sandren acknowledged. "I'd like to accompany you on the *Raven*, but I think it's best if I stay home for this one to keep an eye on things. We're keeping the colonel's past subversion very need-to-know, and he's requested I shadow him to look for any out-of-place behavior."

"Not a bad idea," Kyle assessed. "Based on what we saw from the chancellor while we were on Valta, these aliens are not to be underestimated."

"As for us," Ari chimed in, "what's the entry plan?"

Kira and Sandren talked the team through the strategy they'd devised with Kaen, Leon, and Doctor Elric. The combination of covert ops, science, and pure luck would be a challenge to pull off, but overcoming such odds was part of what made her job so thrilling.

"How much assistance will Ellen be able to offer from the inside?" Nia asked when they were finished with the explanation. "Kyle and I can override the locks, sure, but people are going to see those doors open, even if we're in stealth armor. And Ellen is a visitor there, herself. Can she really clear the way?"

"I could put someone under my direct control," Kira suggested.

Sandren shook his head. "No, save your abilities for dealing with the chancellor. The less they see you in action before that encounter, the better."

Kira nodded. "Understood, sir."

"Sir, back to my point about the infiltration…" Nia cut in. "What kind of help can we expect?"

Sandren folded his hands. "We haven't been able to communicate with Ellen since she went undercover, but she may not be perceived as an outsider. After all, she was originally sent to work with the Elusians *by* Mysarans."

"Yes," Kira conceded, "but as far as Mysarans would be concerned, Ellen defected. She was sent to assassinate the Elusian president, and... well, he's still alive. Plus, she's now publicly his press secretary."

"Well, the Guard's supposed information leak changed the assassination plan," Sandren pointed out. "She didn't have the opportunity to kill him, or so she could say. Besides, Kaen was her contact, not anyone on Mysar. As far as the rest of the government is concerned, she was following his orders, and he may have instructed her to back off. She can go back to her original group and say she wants to return to the good work they were doing and now has a better position to leverage toward that end."

Nia's jaw went slack. "I think we missed some things."

Kira sighed. "Yeah, I'll fill you in while we're in transit."

"All of that aside, counting on an untrained, non-military contact for such a dangerous undercover operation is a big risk, sir," Kyle cautioned.

"Right, but she's all we have." Sandren looked around the table. "I don't think we can trust *anyone* in the Mysaran government right now."

"All right, so we only rely on ourselves to get in and get out," Ari said with his usual assurance. "Simple."

"I have every confidence you'll pull it off." The major smiled. "You leave in an hour."

— — —

Having full control of his own body again was deeply satisfying in a way Kaen could never have imagined, but part of him felt empty. As much as he'd detested Nox's presence, he'd become accustomed to having a companion in his mind.

Though he'd only been consciously aware of Nox for a matter of days, the alien's time as a hidden passenger for the three years prior had left a lasting imprint.

How could such a clear invasion of my mind be something I miss? Kaen shook his head. No, it wasn't that he missed Nox, it was that he had become used to having constraints around his consciousness—in the way that a newborn enjoyed being swaddled. He was now his own person again and he needed to embrace his independence.

Moreover, he wasn't alone. The reason he temporarily felt isolated was that Nox had forced him to withdraw from those who'd always rounded out his life—his friends in the Guard. To regain a sense of fullness, he only needed to reintegrate himself.

Kaen smiled at the thought of being able to participate in those relationships again without an unseen force manipulating him behind the scenes. Good times were ahead in the coming months and years.

In the meantime, though, there were loose ends to tie up.

Two of the three Guard soldiers he'd interviewed had willingly betrayed the Taran Empire, but the third—Alan, the comm tech—was the victim of Nox's subversion. Kaen immediately put in a recommendation for Alan's sentencing to be overturned.

As soon as he was finished, Kaen headed for Leon's lab. He suspected the young scientist already had designs on further research into the alien tech, but it was important to set some ground rules.

Leon was talking with his two associates. They cut off their conversation as soon as they saw Kaen.

"Sir, what can we do for you?" Leon asked.

"I wanted to thank you again for helping to break the

alien's hold over me," Kaen replied.

"Of course, Colonel. I only wish we'd known sooner." Leon studied him. "Doctor Elric and I believe we have calibrated a scan to make it easy to monitor your condition."

"We've adapted that to the routine medical exams for all soldiers to make sure this doesn't happen again," Tess added.

"Good work," Kaen acknowledged. "I take it you've used scans of Jared to test the new systems?"

Leon nodded. "I know he's a prisoner and not a test subject, sir…"

"That's why I'm here," Kaen rested his elbow on the counter of the central workstation. "Regardless of what atrocities Jared helped commit, he's still a person with rights. We can't keep him as an experimental tool for our own gains."

"I would never think of it," Leon replied. "The thing is, though, we can learn things by studying him that we can't gain through any other means."

"I'm well aware. I recognize my former state makes me rather biased, but we need to understand the magnitude of this threat. Can anyone become subverted by touch, or is the procedure more involved?"

"We were just wondering the same thing, sir," Jack said.

Kaen took a slow breath. "I can give you two days to study Jared. That aligns with our vetting time for suspects in any investigation. To continue study beyond that point would violate our ethical codes of conduct."

Leon glanced at his team. "That doesn't give us much time, but we'll make the most of it."

Kaen stepped back toward the door. "Good. I want to know how to take these aliens down."

— — —

Two days would hardly be enough time to run all the testing scenarios he'd like, but Leon was glad they'd be able to use Jared to a positive end after all the harm he'd caused.

After working for hours straight, Leon had his team take a short break. He needed to see Kira off on her mission, and he knew Tess and Jack would work smarter after a power nap.

"How'd your team react to the plan?" Leon asked Kira while he watched her toss items into her travel bag.

"Excited for the thrill of the challenge," she replied. "I still wish Ellen weren't in there. As helpful as she may end up being, I hate having to worry about civilians."

"She can take care of herself pretty well."

"I know resourcefulness runs in your family, but this isn't any old enemy we're up against."

Leon nodded, thinking back about all the times Ellen had talked herself out of tough spots while they were kids. "At least she's adept at mental guards. She's in a better position to protect herself than most would be."

"This is true."

"By the way, we've been given two days to study Jared before we give him the same neural cocktail we used on Kaen. Elric and I should be able to develop an effective treatment for Chancellor Hale once you get her back here, assuming it'll be more difficult than helping the colonel."

"If it's even possible to get the alien presence out of her."

"I thought *I* was supposed to be the skeptical scientist here. Why the 'if'?" Leon asked.

Kira leaned against the wall. "What if the longer the being is in someone, the more difficult it is to remove?"

Leon nodded. "So, we have no way of knowing how long the chancellor has been subverted—or if she's been someone else all along."

"Hale has been the chancellor since we were little kids…"

"Exactly. If she's been an alien that whole time, how much of the original her would be left? She may have been a young woman when she was first taken over, for all we know."

"What would you do in that case?"

"Bring her back here and see if there's anything we can do for her. At a minimum, she'll have information."

Leon took a step toward Kira, seeing the concern in her eyes. "Do they want you to extract that information?"

She shook her head. "I'll do my best to accomplish this op's objectives."

He could see the worry written on her face, but Leon had to acknowledge that Kira shouldn't be going anywhere. Aside from his own feelings about her and his desire to see her safe and secure, the scientist in him recognized that Kira had undergone a major transformation; too much was still unknown about the extent of those changes. She should be under close observation, not out in the field where there were so many variables.

Why is Sandren okay with this? Leon asked himself, though he already knew the answer. Aside from her telepathic skills, Kira was part of a team with unique capabilities related to covert data extraction. The team was stronger when it was intact. Despite Kira's precarious position, it was worth the risk because her going along kept the team together.

All the same, Leon had a responsibility to say what no one else seemed willing to bring up. "I don't like the idea of you going into a dangerous situation like this, Kira. If you started to change—"

"This again? You knew the deal when we agreed to give our relationship another try," Kira shot back.

Her tone stung, even though Leon knew she made a valid

point. He had understood exactly what he was getting into. Kira's career was her first love, no matter how much she cared about him, too. But the circumstances had changed. This wasn't just about her being in the Guard. She, herself, was undergoing a change that transcended job responsibilities or relationship status. Duty may come first, but not at the expense of individual identity.

"I would never stand between you and the Guard, Kira," Leon said in what he hoped was a calm tone. "My concern is that we still know so little about what's going on with you."

"You said yourself that I'm too stubborn to let this thing get the better of me."

"I did, yes."

"So, everything's fine," Kira stated.

"No, it's *not* fine! Colonel Kaen was subverted by some sort of alien parasite, Chancellor Hale is in the same situation, and a rogue telekinetic psychopath made you a medical experiment—"

"Leon," Kira placed her hands on his arms, "I know you mean well, but this isn't helping."

He looked into her hazel eyes. "I don't think it's unreasonable for me to be concerned."

"No, it's not, but I haven't had any transformations since that one. I can't live the rest of my life on a *maybe*. My life here is about taking action, and I adjust when I have to. Right now, the Guard needs me out there with my team."

Leon looked down. "I didn't mean to stop you. I'm just afraid of what may happen when you're put in a stressful situation. Those are the kind of circumstances where something in you could trigger."

"I appreciate your concern, but let me worry about me. Study my nanites when you finish with Jared."

"All right," Leon agreed. "But promise me you'll be careful."

Kira gave him a kiss. "I always am."

— — —

A wave of heat struck Ellen as soon as the shuttle door opened. She blinked as the dry air hit her eyes.

I'd forgotten how hot it can get here in the summer. She walked down the shuttle's ramp onto the landing platform next to the Mysaran capital building.

Unlike the glass tower housing the Elusian government, the Mysaran capital building was only two stories and hewn of black stone. The higher temperature from the planet's proximity to the sun dictated architecture to match the extreme landscape.

Elusia, as a cool world rich with sea life, provided the water to sustain Mysar's agricultural industry under massive biodomes. Plant life flourished in the intense sun, when temperature in the domes was regulated. The mutually beneficially arrangement of Elusia providing fish and water while Mysar provided plants and metal ores from the planet's many mines was the foundation of the Elvar Trinary's economy.

Now, though, with Elusia in the Taran Empire, Mysar was facing a future on its own—a future that wouldn't be sustainable with their current operations.

Ellen had sworn allegiance to Elusia and the Empire, but she still cared about her Mysaran neighbors. She'd gone to school on the planet and had many friends still living there with young families of their own. If those people were being led by an alien outsider working toward its own twisted ends, then she needed to do everything she could to help stop that menace. It was the only way she could start making up for her deceit.

She looked over the capital building, her jaw set with determination. Inside was an enemy lair, and she had to make an opening for Kira's team to come in to free the Mysaran people.

"Is it always this hot?" Nico asked from next to her.

Ellen glanced at the Elusian president's assistant coming down the ramp behind her. President Joris had entrusted Nico with the secret of Ellen's true mission; he'd rendezvous with the Guard ship once it arrived to serve as a political liaison while Ellen and Kira's team were on the inside. That way, if anything started to go poorly, Nico could give an informal heads up to President Joris rather than having an official Guard communication on the record. After all, the Guard should have no business on Mysar, especially in terms of taking military action. The more communications handled via backchannels, the better.

"Mysar is a veritable hellscape compared to our icy Elusia," Ellen replied to his comment.

"No wonder they have such an attitude problem. I'd be angry all the time in this heat, too." Nico wiped beads of perspiration from his brow with the back of his hand.

"You might be onto something there." Ellen took a step away from the shuttle and turned around. "I'll be in touch as soon as I can. The Guard spaceship should arrive tomorrow."

The young man nodded. "I'll be waiting for them. Good luck." He returned to the shuttle.

Ellen walked toward the government building's entrance while the shuttle took off behind her. Even passing into the building's shadow, the oppressive heat barely lessened.

"Hello," she called to a sentry posted at the entrance. "I'm Ellen Calleti. I'm here to see Dominic Thoreau."

The sentry consulted the HUD on his helmet. "I see you on the list. Reception will direct you inside."

"Thank you." Ellen nodded as she passed by.

The revolving door cycled to allow her inside. She breathed in the cool, conditioned air. It was still at least five degrees warmer than the interior temperatures she was used to on Elusia, but at least her lungs didn't feel like they were burning.

A man and a woman with dark features were seated behind a reception desk directly ahead, and they examined Ellen with interest.

"Hello. Dominic Thoreau should be expecting me," she told them. "I'm Ellen Calleti."

The female receptionist made an entry on her console hidden behind the counter. "Take the elevator on the left down to Sublevel 4. Mr. Thoreau will meet you there."

Ellen inclined her head and walked across the lobby to the elevator door. She pressed the call button. Five seconds later, the elevator doors parted, and she stepped inside.

To her surprise, the elevator's control panel had destinations listed all the way to Sublevel 22. What the Mysarans lacked by way of a skyline, they more than made up for underground.

The elevator zipped to its destination of Sublevel 4 in a matter of seconds, and the doors parted to reveal a well-appointed lobby space complete with hydroponic plants, padded seating, and holographic wall art.

A man with dark hair and blue eyes approached from the left hallway feeding into the lobby. "Ellen, I didn't expect to ever see you back on Mysar."

"Unforeseen developments have forced a change," she

replied. "It's good to see you, Dominic."

"Likewise." Dominic held out his arm. "Come, we'll talk in my office."

She followed him down the tiled hall to an opaque glass door at the end. The office beyond was sleek and modern with a black sofa and glass coffee table near the door, a small conference table, and a wooden desk near the left wall—quite a luxury item on a world with so few trees.

Dominic gestured to the couch, and she took a seat while admiring the viewscreen across the entire side wall. The image was presently set to a tropic seashore.

"Beats staring at a rockface, doesn't it?" Dominic commented.

"That it does," Ellen agreed.

"So, what brings you here?"

"I'm looking for a new way to continue our original work."

Dominic placed his arm along the back of the sofa and crossed his legs. "That plan was undone when Elusia joined the Empire."

"Thus realizing the threat we've feared for the sake of the Elvar Trinary. If we wish to keep the dream of independence alive, this is the time we must act." Ellen mirrored his position on the couch, looking the older man in the eyes. "I've come to aid in those efforts. The question is, do you still hold those same convictions?"

"The Mysaran government has never thought otherwise. It's Elusia that abandoned us."

"Circumstances beyond my control, as you well know," Ellen replied.

"What do you propose?" Dominic asked.

"Well, for starters, we need to make sure the Empire leaves us alone."

"And how do you suggest we do that?"

Ellen smiled as she prepared to tell the lie that was sure to get her back in the Mysarans' favor. "By finally taking out Elusia and claiming this entire system for ourselves."

CHAPTER 17

KIRA SET HER travel bag down on her bunk. Her team's cabin on the *Raven* felt different now that she was leaving Leon behind on Orion Station. She'd been on so many missions recently that the small ship was beginning to feel more like home than her actual cabin, but now someone was waiting for her elsewhere.

The shift didn't alter how she perceived her team or her commitment to the Guard—they would always be her extended family—yet, she now had a new sense of grounding. Someone beyond the people she fought alongside cared for her, and that would make her fight even harder to make sure she made it back home.

Nia entered the cabin, interrupting Kira's thoughts. The soldier cast her a wary glance as she swung her bag onto her bunk above Kira's. "Out of quarantine for good?"

"Who knows? But I hope so."

"How are you feeling?"

"No different than before Valta. That's why this is so frustrating."

Nia nodded. "What was it like to transform?"

"The one time it happened, it was so fast I didn't even feel it. But then... I don't know, something wasn't right. It hurt." Kira sat down on her bunk. "I need the three of you to keep an eye on me."

"We always do."

"This is different. It's a risk for me to come with you. Take care of yourselves first and foremost."

"No one gets left behind, Kira," Nia stated.

"Just..." Kira looked down and took a deep breath. "I couldn't bear it if I inadvertently hurt any of you. You'll use those sedatives if—"

Her friend bent her head to catch Kira's gaze. "It won't come to that. We're all going to get through this mission, just like we always do."

"I know I'm probably worrying about nothing."

"Hey, if your worrying keeps us safe, I have no complaints." Nia smiled. "The guys already headed to the gym. Care to join us?"

"Yes! That's exactly what I need." Kira rose from her bunk, and the two women stepped into the hall.

"I have to admit I'm curious," Nia said while they walked. "You said you don't feel any different right now, but have your new nanites impacted you in other ways?"

"You mean like strength and speed augments?"

The soldier nodded.

Kira shrugged. "I did notice a change when I went to the gym earlier, but I don't know to what extent. I guess you'll have to test me."

"I believe that can be arranged." Nia got a devious glint in her eyes.

They descended the ladder to the recreation deck below.

"Are you kidding me?" Kyle was saying to Ari as the two women approached.

"I shite you not," Ari replied.

"What's this, now?" Kira asked.

Kyle gave a dismissive wave. "Ari was just saying that the video of you dancing down the hall has reached Number One video in three different categories."

Kira raised an eyebrow. "Really, guys? We're worried about the entire system—or sector—getting overrun with bodysnatching aliens, and you're talking about that video?" She rose to her full height. "Which contains *classified footage*, need I remind you."

"The video was scrubbed of anything identifiable, don't worry," Ari replied. "And besides, it's not like we have a lot else to do for the next day while we're in transit."

"Oh, nothing like, say, reviewing the mission brief?" Kira asked.

"It was three paragraphs long. Already read," Kyle said.

"Or memorizing the facility layout," Kira continued.

Ari cast her a sidelong glance. "We don't have one."

Kira crossed her arms. "Fine, then checking over your weapons and armor."

"Done and done." Ari folded his hands in his lap. "I think the real issue is you don't want us talking about the video."

The rest of the team looked at her questioningly.

"We're overdue for a workout. Move!" Kira ordered to change the subject.

"That would be a 'yes'," Kyle whispered to Ari, intentionally loud enough for her to overhear.

She ignored them and walked straight ahead to the weight machine. *Oh, revenge is going to be so, so sweet.*

"Back to dodging our questions, Kira?" Ari asked with a

glint in his eyes.

"Oh, don't think for a second I've forgotten about all of your teasing. Your time will come." Kira set the weight machine at slightly above her standard setting and took the bench.

"I'm ready for anything," Ari replied.

"Keep telling yourself that." Kira grabbed the bar on the weight machine and pulled. There may as well have been no resistance at all. "Oh, great."

"Whoa, did you just…?" Kyle commented, catching notice of Kira's attempted workout.

"Okay, so when I said I noticed a change earlier, that may have been an understatement," she admitted.

"Shite, I'll say. It's like there was nothing there." Ari crossed his arms. "How much do you think you can do?"

"I dunno."

Ari and Kyle each grabbed a weight to add to the machine while Nia watched with reserved fascination.

Kira didn't blame her being a little apprehensive. The soldiers were used to Kira barely keeping up with them, not being on the same physical level—or even more.

When the new weights were in place, Kira gave the machine a cautious test pull. She felt more resistance than before, but she still easily pulled the bar to her chest.

"Okay, so not a fluke," she muttered.

"That's fifty percent over your previous personal record," Kyle observed.

"And I'm confident I could double it," Kira replied. "But, I'm not sure I want to. There's no telling when these new nanites might make me freak out. Maybe it's best to leave well enough alone."

"Let's see if you can match my PR, at least," Nia suggested.

Kira nodded her consent.

The two men added additional weights to the machine. Such quantities had always struck Kira as comical when she viewed it as an outside observer, but now she was struck with a mixture of excitement and apprehension at the thought of mastering those weights herself.

If I can do this, then I'll no longer be the weakest one on the team. But is that power worth the uncertain future? Kira gripped the handholds and pulled.

Nothing happened. Or, it didn't feel like it.

"Uh, Kira…" Kyle backed away from her along with the other members of the team.

"Ah, shite." Her mouth felt strange to her.

Then, the pain hit.

Kira's limbs burned, and her fingers felt like they were splitting apart. Her pulse pounded in her ears, blocking out everything except for the burning throughout her body.

At the edge of her consciousness, she felt herself collapse to her hands and knees on the deck. She gaped at the silvery claws starting to extend from her fingertips. The skin on her arms had also taken on a metallic sheen, which darkened as tiny beads of a metallic liquid flowed up through her skin. The pools of shiny liquid crystalized into interlocking scales, creating a second skin above her flesh that was also somehow fused with her senses as though it was her own.

She glanced behind her and saw that Ari had a syringe in his hand. He was inching toward her while Kyle and Nia came around her other side.

"No, don't," Kira managed through labored breaths. "I need to control it."

She still had her mental faculties about her, there was that. If she could think like herself, then there had to be a way to

control the transformation, at least to an extent. But the pain…
Is it getting worse?

The previous time, she hadn't even realized she'd transformed until after it happened. Now, even seemingly after the transformation was complete, the pain persisted. Something was most definitely wrong.

"Argh!" Kira forced herself upright into a kneeling position, willing her heartrate and breathing to normalize. She pictured the peaceful forests of Valta, serene spacescapes, a delicate flower—rotating through the images that helped her center her mind when she needed to concentrate.

Slowly, the pain receded. She watched her talon-like hands as she continued to sit on the floor, waiting to shift back to her normal self. *You have this. You're in control,* she kept repeating to herself. *You're still you.*

The scales and claws dissolved, absorbing back into her skin. She marveled at how the augmentations seemingly merged back inside her. *Is it the nanites themselves?*

She hadn't been able to appreciate the wonder before due to her fear and anger over the unbidden changes. But taking a moment to process the experience now, she felt as though she'd just witnessed something special that demanded her respect, even if it was still terrifying.

"Well, shite." Ari whistled through his teeth. "You weren't exaggerating before."

Nia swallowed. "I'm not sure which part was more unnerving."

Kira rose to her feet. "Sorry about that."

Kyle worked his mouth for a moment. "You were still yourself. You didn't lose control."

"Yeah, maybe we don't have anything to worry about, after all," Nia said.

Just because I haven't doesn't mean that I won't. Kira kept the thought to herself, knowing it wouldn't do anyone any good to dwell on negative scenarios. She needed to maintain a positive outlook. To that end, she elected to also keep the discomfort she'd experienced during the transformation to herself.

"Ari, thank you for being ready to do what needed to be done," Kira told the lance corporal.

He nodded. "I'm glad it wasn't necessary."

"Me, too." She looked over the other members of her team. They still looked understandably nervous, but they were decidedly less tense in appearance than they had been a minute prior. "Well, I think I'll pass on the rest of that workout."

Nia eyed her. "Yeah, I was thinking that might be the case."

"You go ahead and finish yours," Kira told her team. "I'll—"

"Nonsense," Kyle interrupted. "We all got in a good set earlier today. We should do something else together. It's been days since we've been able to have some fun as a team."

"What about Fastara?" Ari suggested.

Kyle and Nia both groaned loudly.

"You're only suggesting that because you weren't horribly beaten," Nia said.

Kira caught on. "Oh, did you play with Leon?"

Kyle glared at her. "He's a menace to civilized society."

"Told us he was an amateur," Nia grumbled.

"Yeah, he's one of the best," Kira said with a chuckle. "I'd say I should have warned you, but Ari's video channel on the Net is a bit too populated with footage of me to have much sympathy for you enduring an embarrassing defeat."

"At least we have a fighting chance against you," Kyle told her.

Kira cracked a smile. "We'll see about that."

— — —

The specifics of Ellen's plan for how to take out Elusia were vague at best, but for the purposes of her conversation with Dominic, details didn't matter. It was the spirit of her words that carried the heft—precisely the message Dominic wanted to hear, tailor-made just for him.

He nodded with satisfaction as Ellen finished her explanation, just as she'd hoped he would.

"I have to say, I was unsure of where your allegiance landed after how the last couple of weeks have played out," he told her.

"I understand your reservations," she replied. "This was the soonest I could make it back here. I thought it was prudent to maintain my position on Elusia to further our long-term objectives."

"Foresightful, indeed." Dominic nodded.

"As I indicated, this next phase will take some careful maneuvering so as not to draw the Taran Empire's wrath."

"That might be an overly melodramatic characterization." Dominic leaned back on the couch. "The Empire is too far-reaching to have much affection for any one planet, especially a tiny border world."

"But we're their newest 'victory'," Ellen stated, wanting to throw him off-balance so she could drive him toward her real objective. "You've heard how the High Dynasty Heads talk about inclusion and democracy and all that. Worlds like Elusia are their symbol for the new-and-improved post-Priesthood society. I suspect they would take extra care to make sure that beacon of hope isn't extinguished before its time."

Dominic looked horrified. "If that's the case, Mysar can never pull away—"

Ellen forced a laugh. "Oh, Dominic, always so serious! Did

you really believe the Empire's interest in this system was genuinely driven by a desire for unity?" She shook her head. "No, this has never been about Elusia. It always comes back to Valta."

He nodded thoughtfully, relaxing again. "Yes, of course. Mysar and Elusia just happen to be the two baggage-worlds that come with the system. Either join or get out of the way."

"Exactly. Elusia, in their infinitely shortsighted weakness, thought that joining would keep them safe, but the Empire will undoubtedly strip Valta and leave the rest of us here to rot."

"Not if we take action." The fire was back in Dominic's eyes.

"There isn't much time," Ellen urged.

"I'd hoped that we could come to a peaceable solution where Elusia could survive, but you're right. This is the only way." Dominic rose from the couch. "We'll need to present the plan to the chancellor for approval."

"Would you like me to write a brief?" Ellen offered.

"No need. Come with me and you can present it yourself."

Ellen's pulse spiked. "I wasn't expecting to meet with the chancellor directly." *Shite! That's probably the most powerful telepath of them all. How are my mental guards supposed to stand up to that?*

If she was to be honest with herself, she knew they wouldn't. She also recognized that she'd made a huge error in her assumptions about how events would proceed on Mysar. Her plan had always been to use Dominic as an intermediary. To be asked to communicate directly with the chancellor was an honor, but it also exponentially increased her personal risk.

"You've put a lot of thought into this. You deserve some facetime with the top decision-maker," Dominic told her.

"Thank you, that means a lot," Ellen lied. *I should have*

anticipated this possibility. This is what I get for rushing in.

Chastising herself wouldn't change the present situation, though, so she set the thought aside.

"Come with me." Dominic led her out of his office.

The location of the chancellor's council chambers were well-known to Ellen from her previous time working in the Mysaran government building, but the location seemed much more confined within the structure now that she wasn't confident she'd have a clear path out.

She and Dominic took the elevator up to Level 2 above the surface, and then passed through several administrative wings within the squat government building before they arrived at the outer entrance to the chancellor's chambers. Guards waited outside the doors—the only armed guards Ellen had seen beyond those posted at the outer entrance—and they stiffened when she approached.

"Name and appointment?" the guard on the right asked.

"Dominic Thoreau. I don't need an appointment," he replied.

The guard conferred with a screen mounted next to the door. "Go ahead."

The second guard swung the entry door open so Ellen and Dominic could enter.

Inside, a spacious anteroom was furnished with two ornate couches facing one another, a coffee table between them, and sophisticated artwork around the walls. The most notable feature of the room, however, was a bank of broad windows along the right wall—a rare luxury outside one of the biodomes.

Ellen looked upon the furnishings with a suitable level of admiration without gawking, to which Dominic responded with a knowing smile.

"This is your chance to enter the Mysaran elite, Ellen. Loyal civil servants can go far."

The loyalty part was where she was going to run into trouble, at least when it came to *which* master she pledged to. She nodded. "I'm here to serve."

Dominic took a seat on the couch with a view out the window, and Ellen sat down beside him.

As soon as they were settled, a door on the back wall, to Ellen's left, opened, and the Mysaran chancellor emerged.

Cynthia Hale had a strong presence about her, even from a distance. Knowing what she did now, Ellen wondered if that stemmed from the alien controlling her or if it was that spark that had attracted the alien to Hale as a host in the first place.

Ellen and Dominic rose out of respect when the chancellor entered, and she gave them a nod.

"Chancellor, thank you for taking a meeting without notice," Dominic said. "I just had a rather intriguing conversation with Ellen here, and I think you'd be interested in what she has to say."

Hale's gaze turned to Ellen as she gracefully lowered herself to the couch across from the two visitors.

Ellen could feel the older woman skim her mind. *I serve Mysar. Elusia stands in our way,* she thought to herself as a cover for her inner thoughts. She wasn't sure her mental guards would hold up to intense scrutiny, but she may as well put up the best show she could.

The chancellor lingered for several moments, and then Ellen felt her mental presence withdraw. "And who are you, Ellen?"

"Ellen Calleti, ma'am. I'm from Valta, but I attended school here on Mysar. I began working with the government as an intern, and I quickly realized Mysar's culture more closely aligned with my own ways of thinking than my homeworld."

"Yet, you are now the Elusian president's new press secretary, correct?" Hale raised an eyebrow.

Ellen nodded. "A little over two years ago, I was approached by the Sovereign. I was sent to Elusia to get close to the administration so that I could kill the president, should the need arise."

"I am quite familiar with this organization and the intent," Hale revealed. "I'm the one who wrote their mission statement."

Ellen had suspected as much, but she was surprised the chancellor would be so candid. "A cause I believe in, ma'am. I'm still upset that the president moved forward with rejoining the Empire so quickly. I didn't have a chance to act."

"You maintained your close place. Why?" the chancellor asked.

"That's why I invited Ellen here to speak with you," Dominic interjected. "She presented a plan that would give Mysar permanent independence."

Ellen nodded. "In my time working on Elusia, I had contact with a covert ops group within the Tararian Guard. I learned through those interactions that the Empire is somewhat selective about the matters they get involved in. A world such as Elusia doesn't have much to offer and, therefore, will take a lower priority when it comes to dealing with potential issues. If Mysar were to make a direct move against Elusia, the Empire could easily overwhelm us, wipe us out. But what we want is for the entire system to be left alone. We need to make the Empire distrust Elusia itself. If the Empire decides Elusia should not be a member, they'd leave and never come back."

Hale nodded. "And I take it you have a strategy to make that happen?"

"I do. Now, what could little Elusia do that would be a threat to the Taran Empire?" Ellen asked rhetorically.

Hale glanced at Dominic, then gave Ellen a questioning look.

"You threaten the thing that allows them to maintain control over their domain: the navigation beacon network," Ellen continued. "Make it look like Elusia is trying to hack the beacon outside the Elvar Trinary—to have any transit to the system be on their terms. After such tampering, effective or not, the Empire will assume Elusia was disingenuous in their intentions about the free and open exchange of resources as a member world, and they'll withdraw."

The chancellor leaned back on the couch. "That is a very interesting plan, indeed."

— — —

Leon and Doctor Elric studied the monitor inlaid in the lab's wall. Having Jared in custody offered too great a research opportunity to waste any time during the two days they were authorized to study him.

"What's next?" Leon asked the Guard doctor.

"This is your lab, I'm just here as a consultant," Elric replied.

"You know the Guard's operations, though. I'm an outsider." Leon turned back to the tray where they had the sample of the live nanites collected from Jared.

They had an array of chemicals on hand to add to the sample to gauge reactions. It was how they had determined the baseline mixture to give Kaen, but Leon was interested to see what would happen if they went the opposite direction with the dosing.

To maintain as much scientific rigor as possible, they had been adding controlled amounts of the chemicals in sequential order. The findings supported their initial observations that neurochemicals associated with positive emotional experience suppressed this particular strain of nanites while those linked with sadness or aggression fueled the nanite's functions.

Leon was particularly interested to find out how the nanites behaved when introduced into a new host. Of course, they couldn't actually expose a person to the nanites, so his study was restricted to what he could observe in test batches and within Jared. Unfortunately, the time with their subject was running down far too quickly.

Doctor Elric eased into one of the tall chairs at the workstation. "I'm used to dealing with Taran technology—and even some newly rediscovered tech from the Aesir—but this," he pointed to the graphic on the screen, "is something else entirely. It's all disjointed."

"What could it mean?" Leon asked.

The doctor took a deep breath. "If I had to speculate, I'd say that this race has adopted pieces from different sources and cobbled it together."

"That means that there are other aliens out there."

"Likely, but we've always suspected that," Elric continued.

"At any rate, how do we fight these guys?" Leon pointed at the screen. "We think they're in Gaelon, but if they have no bodies, what do we look for?"

"There is that issue, yes."

Leon nodded. "It concerns me that their base may be so close to my home system."

"On the flip side, that proximity is what made your home

the way it is," the doctor said. "We know the tech is alien in origin, yet it's markedly similar to seemingly naturally occurring neural structures in native Valtans. Add in that your people in the Elvar Trinary never venture into Gaelon despite it being the neighboring system, and the entire situation sounds like a conspiracy orchestrated by this master race."

"Especially since we know they have embedded themselves in the Mysaran government."

"Precisely."

Leon thought for a moment. "We need to learn more about the nanotech's mode of transmittal."

"Agreed. I'd like to be certain we won't have new subverted officers walking around with no notice."

"No kidding."

"In the meantime," Elric continued, "I think I have enough data to devise a vaccine, of sorts, to prevent the nanites from being able to create a TR."

"That's a major step forward." Leon paused. "What do we say about the nature of the nanotech?"

The doctor shrugged. "It's alien and it's dangerous. We can treat the symptoms here, but to stop the menace, they'll have to go to the source. Once Kira's team gets the chancellor, we'll know where that is."

CHAPTER 18

THE *RAVEN* DROPPED into orbit around Mysar in full stealth mode. Kira had been on a number of missions that required a silent approach, but never before had she gone after a world leader.

"I'll check in with Colonel Kaen. Stand by," Kira instructed her team and then headed to the private communications booth.

Kaen answered her video call after ten seconds. "What's your status?"

"Just arrived, sir."

"Excellent. President Joris relayed information about the transport ship Ellen used to get to Mysar. One of his administrative assistants, named Nico, is waiting for you at the spacedock. He can provide the specifics."

Information appeared on the screen detailing how to contact the Elusian ship. "Understood, sir."

"You have clearance to use Nico as a point of contact while you're on the surface, and he can relay information back to us. The encrypted signals will draw less attention if they're going to a known ship."

"Can he be trusted, sir?"

"I have the Elusian president's word."

Considering that President Joris trusted Ellen and she was an assassin sent to kill him, I'm not sure the man is a great judge of character. Kira nodded. "We'll use our best discretion for communications."

"Good luck on the surface. I'll be awaiting your report." Kaen terminated the comm link.

Kira sighed. *This entire op is a shiteshow through and through.*

She was used to improvising and adapting to situations with questionable intel, but the combination of complications in this case were starting to add up. Even though she was never one to back down from a challenge, there were many more lives than her own on the line.

After taking a minute to clear her head, Kira opened an encrypted channel with Nico's transport ship.

The video feed resolved on the wall-mounted viewscreen. A young man was seated at a communication station similar to her own. "You must be Kira," he stated. "I know communicating through an intermediary isn't ideal, but it was the best solution Ellen and I could come up with on short notice."

"That's what happens when you don't think through a plan! You should have left this to the Guard."

"I wasn't a part of that decision." Nico spread his hands on the tabletop. "What I *can* tell you is how Ellen will facilitate your access to the government building."

"I'm listening."

He cleared his throat. "So, Ellen used to work closely with a man named Dominic when she was employed as a Mysaran administrator. As I understand it, he officially holds a place in the Mysaran government, but he's the main liaison with the underground group responsible for all the advocacy for Mysaran independence, the Sovereign. The government pulls the strings for the actions this group carries out. He got Ellen her place in the Elusian Alliance."

Kira eyed him.

"Yes, I'm aware of why she was originally sent to Elusia," Nico revealed. "The president granted her an official pardon, and I processed the executive order."

"And you still trust her coming back here?"

He nodded. "I spoke with her at length during the trip over. She's changed her thinking. I believe in the right for people to learn and grow."

"I agree." Kira paused. "All right, so she's convinced Dominic that she wants in again. How does that help my team get to the chancellor?"

"Because the Sovereign collaborate more closely with the government than most realize—even those who know about the arrangement. Dominic, and now Ellen by extension, regularly lets members of the Sovereign into the capital building for strategy meetings. They have a back entrance for that occasion, and it's the only time the security system is deactivated, so there isn't an official record. Ellen will have access to that meeting schedule and can tell you exactly where to go to avoid the security system."

Kira crossed her arms. "That's great, and all, but we have stealth suits. We need to get down there as soon as possible, not wait for one of these meetings to happen."

"There's one tonight."

"Oh."

"Ellen sent me a datapacket with the details," Nico continued. "Would you like me to forward it?"

"Okay, I have to admit, that will be helpful, but this doesn't forgive the fact that she ran in without clearing her plan with the Guard."

"You can bring that matter up with her yourself in…" Nico checked the time, "three hours. She'll be waiting for you at the entrance to the council chambers."

An indicator on the screen blinked as the datapacket transferred to the *Raven*.

"Thanks, Nico. I'll have the crew relay any relevant information once we're down in the field. Be prepared to rendezvous back at Elusia."

"We'll be standing by. May the stars be with you."

— — —

The meeting with the chancellor had gone surprisingly well. Chancellor Hale had asked Ellen precisely the right questions to show that she was engaged with her idea. Everything seemed to be going to plan.

Now seated in the back corner of a room filled with cubicles, Ellen assessed her work station and surroundings. *How closely will they be monitoring my communications?*

If nothing else, she needed to look the part a Sovereign loyalist while she waited for the Guard to arrive. She made coded notes about her meeting with the chancellor, using the organization's secret vernacular. Everything was presented as official Mysaran government business using a code, so a discussion of a new water pipeline could really be a conversation about positioning mercenaries to seize an Elusian supply cache.

When she'd completed the plan overview, Ellen peeked over the edge of her cubicle to see if any of her coworkers were paying attention to her. They all appeared to be absorbed in their work.

I better do this while I have the chance. Ellen took a deep breath and began the riskiest part of her venture yet.

It was one thing to lie to a person but quite another to try to fool a computer. Though piggybacking a personal message on an official communication was as challenging as it was risky, it was critical she confirm the details about the Sovereign's meeting schedule for Nico so he could relay the information to the Guard. Assuming they received the information, the Guard team should land on the planet in another hour.

There was nothing more for Ellen to do before then. *Now how should I look busy?*

Approaching footfalls drew her attention. Ellen craned her neck to see who was coming. To her horror, she saw three guards wearing body armor.

Oh, shite! She ducked back into her cubicle. Being in the back corner, she had nowhere to run except straight past the approaching guards. *Did that latest communication give me away?*

Her mind raced, trying to think of how she'd explain her actions. She held her breath while she prayed to the stars that the guards weren't coming for her. Of course, she couldn't be so lucky.

The three soldiers turned down her aisle. Two stopped three meters from her while the other continued ahead until he blocked the entrance to her cube.

"Ellen Calleti." It was a statement not a question.

She swallowed. "Is there a problem?"

The burly man scoffed. "That depends on whether or not you want to cooperate."

"I'm here as a servant to the Mysaran government. Why wouldn't I?"

The guard shook his head. "It really didn't take long for you to confirm our suspicions."

"I don't know what you're talking about," Ellen insisted, even as an icy chill gripped her chest.

"Did you think we were that stupid? That you could contact an Elusian ship without us knowing?"

Ellen bristled. "Yes, of course I'm communicating with that ship! I was sent here on official Elusian business, and I need to keep up appearances. I have a designated contact on that vessel. I wasn't hiding anything from you."

The guard consulted with the colleagues. Another guard nodded.

"All the same," he continued, "we need to take you in for further questioning. Standard procedure. If you have nothing to hide, then you don't have anything to worry about."

"Have you talked to Dominic about this?"

"He's the one who requested we take you in," the guard replied.

Ellen's heart dropped. "He—"

"Well, it wasn't me, exactly," Dominic said, coming up behind the guards.

She pivoted to address him. "I just got here! Why are you—"

"Oh, Ellen." Dominic leaned against the cubicle divider of an adjacent workspace. "You honestly believed you could get back in with us this easily?"

"I was loyal—"

"Oh, at the time, yes," he agreed. "But we know you're one of the Elusians now. We're not sure who you're working with, precisely, but this was all a ploy to gather information, no?"

"Dominic, you know me."

"I *knew* you, Ellen. But you are no longer the young woman I mentored. Whatever happened on Elusia was not a setback to our plans. You turned against us. When you showed back up here with that bold plan, I suspected you weren't being genuine with your motivations. Only the chancellor could determine if your intentions were honest, so she read you. And Ellen, you have not been very forthcoming." Dominic locked her in a piercing stare.

Ellen's heart pounded in her ears. *I thought the Guard would get here before they realized...*

She should have known her cover was blown the moment she went to meet with the chancellor. Of course, she'd never get an audience like that, regardless of the plan she had presented. Dominic had been playing her the whole time.

"What happens now?" she asked, realizing it was pointless to resist. Being too obstinate might make them inclined to kill her on the spot, but if she feigned cooperation, perhaps she'd be able to buy herself time until the Guard arrived.

Dominic scoffed. "What do *you* think will happen, Ellen? We'll learn what we can from you, and then it'll end for you the same way it ends for anyone who opposes us."

Yeah, with that kind of thinking, no wonder people have a tendency to defect. It was a little late for that sentiment. If they had already pegged her as a traitor, she may as well play up that story to make herself seem valuable enough to keep around for a while longer.

"Yes, I was sent here to relay information back to Elusia," Ellen admitted.

"Ah, finally some honesty." Dominic perked up.

His willingness to believe the lie revealed a valuable piece of information to Ellen: he wasn't subverted by one of the aliens, at least not under permanent control. She might be able to slip some little lies through. *I'll see how long I can keep them off the Guard's trail.*

Dominic took a step toward her. "You know, that's the only reason we didn't arrest you the moment you walked into my office. There was no way you'd come here completely alone, so it was more advantageous to wait until you directly implicated your co-conspirators."

"This opposition is bigger than a handful of individuals," Ellen shot back.

"Then it's helpful that our definition of victory calls for total dominance."

Ellen swallowed. "Have you ever taken a step back to ask why? Do you know who you're working for?"

"That's why it's always been such an easy decision," Dominic replied. "We are such simple, mortal creatures. How could we not answer to such superior beings?"

"They've brainwashed you."

He chuckled. "Oh, no. They've been kind enough to show us how much better we can become."

Ellen stared at him with disbelief. "Is that all that Mysar is now? A planet dedicated to helping some outside race exert its superiority?"

"It's not like we won't get anything in return." He smiled. "We're so close to being able to turn our simple race into the soldiers we were meant to become. The ancient technology has been there, and they took it and built upon it. With their intellect and our physical forms, we will rise."

"I think you're underestimating your opposition."

Dominic cocked his head. "If they want a fight, then let them bring it."

— — —

"All right, team, we have everything we need to complete this op without coming under fire," Kira said while she loaded into the landing shuttle with Ari, Kyle, and Nia.

"Then why do we have the big guns?" Kyle asked with a smirk.

"Because we're totally going to get shot at," Ari said loudly while cupping his hand over his mouth to mime a whisper.

Kira chuckled. "You know the drill."

Nia took the shuttle's controls next to Kira. "What happens if we get captured?" she asked.

The team didn't broach the topic too often, even on the riskiest missions. Though there were official protocols on the books, each situation called for a tailored approach, given the relative likelihood of backup arriving, the sensitivity of the information they were sent in to extract, or other factors. They were all prepared to give their lives in the line of duty, but facing that possible mortality was always different than the hypotheticals.

"We don't get caught," Kira told the lance corporal. "There's no reason all of us won't walk out of there."

Nia nodded. "Yes, ma'am."

Kira kept her own nerves to herself, knowing that expressing her misgivings about their ill preparation wouldn't help her team. At least Nico had relayed Ellen's confirmation of the landing plan. That part was on track, if nothing else.

When everyone was strapped in, Kira powered up the shuttle. "Here we go!"

The shuttle dropped out of the *Raven*'s belly and then boosted at an angle toward the planet as soon as it was clear of the craft. Its stealth tech would make the craft almost impossible to spot during its descent.

Kira and the rest of her team remained silent for the initial approach, their gazes fixed out the viewports to get the lay of the land.

"It's so barren," Nia commented once they were low enough that details in the landscape began to come into focus. "I can't imagine why anyone would settle here when Valta was an option."

"To each their own, I guess." Kira said.

The shuttle set down behind a rock outcropping a kilometer from the capital building. Kira and the team moved to the back of the shuttle and checked their stealth armor.

"Everyone ready?" she asked.

"All set," the three soldiers acknowledged.

"And you have the...?" Kira prompted.

They all patted compartments on their hips containing a sedative.

"We won't need it, but we're ready," Nia assured her.

Kira secured the shuttle while the others scrambled up the side of the surrounding rock outcropping to get eyes on their destination. She joined them on the lip of the ridge. "How's it look?"

"Clear, as far as we can tell," Ari replied.

"Then let's go," Kira ordered.

The four soldiers loped across the harsh landscape, keeping to the shadows of rocks as much as possible. Stealth armor or not, there was no need to run right out in the open in case the enemy had some means of spotting them.

They covered the single kilometer quickly. As they neared their destination of the back-entry door, Kira motioned for Ari to take point and scope out their final approach. She waited with the other two members of the team behind a boulder.

"Two guards are posted outside," Ari reported into his comm. "There's cover on the approach. We should be able to get close enough for a sonic blast."

"Do it. We'll cover you."

Ari slipped ahead while Kira jogged along several meters back with Nia and Kyle to either side. They darted to the various rocks along the way.

When he reached the boulder closest to the door, Ari took cover and aimed his multi-handgun at the two guards, set to sonic stun. He fired.

The two guards dropped to the ground.

Kira ran forward with her weapon drawn in case additional guards emerged from the building. "Okay, time to find out if that code Ellen gave us for the door works." She located the access panel and keyed in the code.

Nothing happened.

She tried it again. A red light illuminated.

Shite! She glanced at the other members of the team. "Kyle, think you can crack it?"

He hesitated. "Sure, but what does it mean that *this* information was wrong?"

More than Kira wanted to admit. "We proceed with the mission."

"All right." Kyle jogged forward, drawing the compact device he used to interface with computer terminals. He synced with the keypad.

"I don't like this," Ari muttered under his breath.

"This reeks of a trap," Nia added. She tightened her grip on her weapon.

"We'll fight our way in if we have to." Kira pressed her back against the side wall, ready for action.

"Almost got it," Kyle said. "There!"

The light on the access panel turned blue, and the bolt unlocked with a clang. Kyle swung the door open with one hand while aiming his weapon inside with the other.

Ari ran up behind him, staring down his sights. "Looks clear," he reported, then paused. "Did you hear that?"

Kira listened. "Shite, they're coming!"

CHAPTER 19

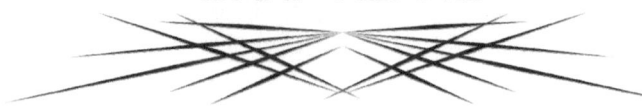

KIRA MOTIONED HER team backward around the cover of the building. "Hold your fire."

She listened to the swift footfalls in the hallway, halting just inside the door.

"Do any of you have line of sight on the enemy?" she asked her team over their comms.

"Negative," Ari replied. "I can see where they found cover, though."

Fok, there's no way to handle this without making a scene. She took a deep breath. "Toss in a flash grenade."

Kyle glanced at her. "That will give away our posi—"

"Do it!"

Ari pulled out a grenade from his belt and activated it. "Not like they don't already know we're here." He tossed it inside.

The hallway was bathed in white light as the flash grenade detonated. The guards inside stumbled from their hiding places, dazed.

Kira and her team fired into the hall, striking the guards with sonic blasts. Half a dozen guards dropped to the floor.

A volley of kinetic rounds buzzed past Kira.

"Back to cover!" she ordered.

Kyle and Nia took the left side of the entry door while Kira and Ari braced themselves on the right wall.

"This is off to a *great* start." Nia assessed the enemy's positions on her HUD. "Six disabled, another four firing from seventeen meters back."

Kira confirmed the survey on her own HUD. "We need to secure a position inside."

"The air is clear when they aren't firing. They won't be able to see us in the stealth suits," Kyle observed.

"Not until we're right on top of them." Kira crept into the corridor.

The drywall along the hallway was now pitted from the kinetic rounds. Better the walls than her armor.

She picked her footing carefully around the unconscious guards, jogging between the minimal cover afforded by recessed doorways.

Kira tried the handle on the first door she encountered, but it was locked. *All right, straight ahead it is.* She advanced, trying each door with the same result. By the time she reached the final door, she was a mere three meters from the four guards hiding in a hallway T-intersection.

There was no way to get a direct shot, but she could see her targets just beyond her sightlines.

"I'm going for it," she told her team.

Without hesitation, she sprinted forward, firing a perfectly aimed sonic blast into the right-hand hallway as she passed through the intersection.

The four guards dropped to the floor before they knew what hit them.

"All right, that worked rather well," Kyle admitted over the comm.

"Not exactly a best practice, but whatever works." Kira edged back to the intersection and looked down. The HUD showed the way was clear. "Let's find a communication room. The original plan is off. We need to find out what went wrong."

They made their way down the hallway, scouting for an access terminal. Eventually, Nia spotted a dataport.

Kyle initiated an interface and burrowed into the system. "There's a communications room about ninety meters away, down a couple corridors to the left." He sent the map to the team's shared HUD overlay.

"Looks like a pretty easy route," assessed Ari.

"That's our best bet to get deeper into the database," Nia said. "If we can get to that room, we can likely procure all the access codes we'll need to get into the chancellor's chambers."

"Agreed," Kira said with a nod. "Reinforcements are almost certainly on their way."

Not a moment later and the sounds of scuffling footfalls carried down the corridor.

"Shall we?" Kyle held out his hand in the direction they needed to go.

"Let's test out this stealth tech for real." Kira jogged ahead of her team.

Twenty meters down the hall, she spotted their opposition. Unaware of Kira's stealthed team, the soldiers were in the middle of the corridor, leaving a narrow margin along either side.

Kira continued forward carefully, keeping her footsteps silent. Though her stealth suit was invisible to a casual observer, there was still a risk of her solid form casting shadows, so she didn't want to draw attention from any sudden movements. When she was almost to the soldiers' positions, she pressed herself into the narrow recesses of a doorway. She waited.

The guards passed her by, leaving a clear path down the hall.

"Like a pro," Nia said with an audible smirk.

"Get your asses over here," Kira told her team.

Using her technique, the three other soldiers slipped past the Mysaran guards.

Ari chuckled into the comm. "Poor bastards won't know what to do when they can't find us."

"Let's not get cocky. This is far from over." Kira jogged down the corridor along the course Kyle had indicated on the facility layout.

They saw no other people in the halls on the rest of the way to the communications room, but Kira suspected others must be close.

Outside the communication room itself, Kira used the sensors on her suit to look through the wall. "Two occupants," she told her team.

"Sonic blast may mess with the equipment," Nia cautioned.

"Then we lure them out." Kira beckoned for Kyle to crack the security lock on the door.

"What's your plan?" Nia asked while her colleague worked.

"Stealth tech is great and all, but sometimes to get results, you need to do things the old-fashioned way. Follow my lead." Kira smiled, even though her team couldn't see it.

As soon as the door lock clicked open, Kira stomped her booted foot against the door. It flew open. She deactivated the stealth on her armor and pointed her gun through the door. "On the ground!" she demanded over the external comm.

The two occupants dropped to their knees and then lay down, placing their hands behind their heads.

"See? Easy," Kira said on the private comm channel.

Ari and Kyle grabbed the two techs by their wrists and dragged them into the hall. As soon as they were clear of the sensitive equipment, Ari hit the techs with a sonic blast to knock them out.

"I have to say, I really love this gun." Ari said.

Nia patted him on the shoulder. "Oh, and you handle it so well."

Ari cocked his head. "That sounded dirty."

"Did it? You must be desperate for some attention." Nia sauntered back into the communication room.

Kira sent a private high-five to Nia's HUD.

Ari grabbed the two techs and dragged them back inside the room, closing the door behind him.

"Stealth back on," Kira instructed. "I'll contact the *Raven* to let them know what's going on."

Kyle and Nia immediately got to work hacking into the system.

Kira opened up a secure connection to their ship using the suit's comms. She advised the *Raven*'s captain of the change in plan so he could keep Guard command apprised of the situation.

"Can't say I'm surprised," he replied when she was finished.

"Me either, but we'll adapt. Given that, Nico and the Elusian ship should probably get out of here," Kira advised.

"I'll pass on the message. Be careful down there."

"Talk to you soon." Kira terminated the connection and then joined Ari in standing guard while Kyle and Nia worked.

"We're in," Kyle reported after two minutes.

"Wow, there's some strange stuff going on here," Nia observed while she browsed through the database. "Either they have a *lot* of public infrastructure projects that never get constructed, or there's some sort of code at play. It looks like there's a public-facing part of the government, and then… whatever this is." She pointed at the screen.

"I was thinking the same thing," Kyle agreed. "There's clearly a part of the database that's used for real administration and then another part that's likely related to the work the Mysarans are doing for their alien overlords."

"And you say *I'm* the one with the flare for the dramatic," Ari commented from next to the door.

"The alien overlords are more real than I'd like," Kira interjected.

"Holy shite, yeah, they are!" Kyle exclaimed. "Take a look at this."

Kira read over the text he was pointing to on the screen. "Is that a record of MTech's research projects?"

"Yeah, it is. And half of these projects are using tech that seems to have mysteriously appeared," the soldier explained. "Whatever is going on here, Kira, it's definitely beyond just MTech and the chancellor. The entire government is in on it."

So much for taking out the chancellor and single-handedly eliminating the threat to this system. Kira took a slow breath. "Okay, so how do we determine which members of the government are involved and who's doing the normal business around here?"

"Should we assume there's a distinction?" Nia asked.

"Maybe we can't," Kira realized. "I mean, Ellen didn't know anything was amiss when she was working here."

"So, maybe *all* of the administration is being controlled by the aliens, but that doesn't mean that everyone who's performing those tasks knows what they're doing," Kyle said. "If no one knows any better, anything could be made to look legitimate."

"We'll need to vet everyone after this is over," Kira agreed. "Only a test to look for the TR Leon identified will reveal who's been completely subverted."

"Willing collaborators may be worse," Nia grumbled.

"I can't disagree with that. But I think anyone who's gone along that willingly, knowing what they're doing, will be easy to spot," Kira told her.

"Speaking of collaborators," Kyle interjected, "I think I found out what happened to Ellen, but you're not going to like it."

"Oh, shite." Nia slouched in her chair.

Kira looked at Kyle's terminal. Displayed on the monitor was footage of a woman a few years older than Kira strapped to a chair in a concrete-walled room. "Foking great. Looks like Ellen got herself found out and caught."

"They must have realized she had defected for good," Nia murmured.

"Of course, they did!" Kira groaned. "It was idiotic of her to think she could fool them."

"What do we do?" Kyle asked.

Kira took a slow breath. "First, we go for Ellen. Then the chancellor will have some explaining to do."

— — —

The room was dark and surprisingly cold. Ellen's thoughts were fuzzy, but she knew she was still on Mysar. *I must be somewhere... underground?*

"Ah, you're awake." A female voice pierced the darkness.

"Chancellor?" Ellen questioned, trying to see who'd spoken.

"I have to give you credit for trying," the voice continued. It was decidedly female, but there was an alien quality to the vocalization. Whether it was adrenaline clouding her judgment or something much more deeply rooted, Ellen had the distinct impression that her captor was not the woman with whom she had spoken only hours before.

"What did you think you would accomplish here?" the voice asked.

"If you want me to share my secrets, then at least show your face," Ellen shot back.

"Such vigor! It's a shame you weren't willing to work with us. You could have been such an asset."

"Is that all you have to say?" Ellen flexed her hands, realizing they were bound behind her back.

"I won't ask you again. Why are you here?"

The question was as much in Ellen's mind as she heard it spoken aloud. It bored into her, demanding a response. She tried to fight it, but the compulsion was too strong to resist.

"I'm—I'm here to learn," she stammered.

"Learn what?" the voice snarled in her mind and out loud.

"What you are doing here. So we can stop you."

The voice chuckled. "Of course, you are. The foolish always think we can be stopped, but you never know where to look."

Ellen strained against her restraints in her chair. "If others keep coming for you, I'd think you'd eventually take the hint."

"You really are more spirited than most. Or very stupid. If you truly understood who I am, you'd never speak to me in that tone."

"Then tell me!" Ellen glared into the darkness.

Finally, a light faded on in front of her. The chancellor stepped forward.

"You shouldn't meddle in what you don't understand."

Ellen glared into the woman's pale green eyes. "If you think I have so much potential, then try me. Maybe I'll see it your way if I understand."

The woman stared back. Ellen could feel her assessing her mind. "No, you've already decided. There's no swaying you."

"Then just kill me."

"Oh, no." The chancellor took two more steps forward. "Don't you get it? You're still a Valtan. The rest of you don't have nearly the potential of the Readers, but you'll make a fine Robus."

"What are you talking about?"

Hale cocked her head. "Oh, your friends in the Guard didn't tell you?"

"About what?"

The chancellor laughed. "Oh, Ellen, you're in for quite a surprise when you see Kira again." She stepped forward until she was only a half-meter in front of Ellen, then extended her hand and ran her index finger down Ellen's face. "You'll make a lovely host."

They'll come for me soon. I can get out of this. Ellen tried to keep her thoughts to herself.

A smile touched the chancellor's lips. "Yes, they're already here. But no, Ellen, there will be no escape for you. We've been expecting your friends. It's what we counted on."

CHAPTER 20

KIRA COULDN'T SHAKE the feeling that she and her team were being watched. "These hallways are too empty," she said into her comm.

"It is the end of working hours," Nia replied. "But yeah, I know what you mean."

They had made it out of the wing where they'd initially entered the building and were now traversing a hallway on the ground level that would lead them to a stairwell. The chancellor's administrative chambers were on the second story, but the layout indicated an underground facility beneath them.

According to the information Ellen had passed along, the meeting with the Sovereign would take place in an underground conference space. However, considering that Ellen was now strapped to a chair and Kira's team had been welcomed by armed guards, everything they thought they knew going into the op was clearly bad intel.

Kira had to trust her instincts, and those told her to check the chancellor's office. *This is probably the very trap they want us to walk into, but these aliens are also cocky bastards. The chancellor will want to witness our supposed defeat herself, and that's when we'll get her.*

Four soldiers against an unknown number of Mysaran soldiers would make for difficult odds. However, Kira was confident in her team's superior tech and training.

"Shite!" Kyle froze behind her.

A second later, Kira noticed the issue. The stairwell they were headed for wasn't a closed stairwell the way it had looked on the facility plan—it was actually an open lobby, and it was filled with people.

"Ah, fok." She evaluated the lobby on her HUD, expanding the view to see the upper level. It appeared that the people on the ground level were office workers getting ready to leave for the day, while there were at least two armed guards posted outside a sealed door upstairs, which led to the chancellor's chambers.

"Your orders, ma'am?" Ari prompted.

Kira weighed the options. "We need to get upstairs. The guards are almost certainly looking for us, but I doubt all of these workers are in on it. With the stealth suits, we should be able to slip right through the crowd and walk up the stairs."

"That's... a little crazy," Kyle replied.

"Hiding in plain sight, right?" Kira said. She wasn't sure she believed it, but they didn't have a lot of options. If nothing else, it was unlikely the Mysaran soldiers would open fire in a crowded room. At least, she hoped they wouldn't.

Nia shifted on her feet. "Maybe there's a back way?"

"No, there isn't," Kyle countered. "I don't like this plan, either, but this is our only way up there."

"Problem with one way up is there's only one way back," Ari chimed in. "The chancellor might not even be there."

Kira nodded. "You're right. It's a worthwhile risk if we know we can get to our target, but we don't. Is there any way we can determine the chancellor's position before making a move?"

"That really depends on the computer system," Kyle replied. "If they were expecting us, all of the information we're seeing may be fabricated to tell us what we want to see."

"There has to be *something* that can't be faked," Kira insisted.

Nia tilted her head. "Well, there may be."

Kira turned to her. "What do you have in mind?"

"We can trust the sensors on our suits. We'd have to compare those readings with what we observe on the central computer system," Nia explained.

"I have an idea," Kyle mused.

"I'm all ears," Kira said.

"I think I can patch my suit into the facility's internal security system. Based on what I saw in the communications room earlier, the security authentications aren't very sophisticated. We can use the facility's sensors to collect data, and the suit will reconcile the inputs."

Nia nodded. "Yes, that could work. Reports can easily be doctored, but the sensory processor in our suits can tease out what's real."

"And how does that get us Hale?" Kira asked.

"Oh, you're forgetting how good I am," Kyle replied. "Once we narrow down where she might be, we just look at the video feeds until we see her."

"And if there aren't video cameras in that room?"

"There will at least be a computer or viewscreen with an integrated camera we can activate remotely. If there isn't, then we scan for audio and locate her voice signature."

Kira nodded. "Okay, try it." She followed Kyle back in the direction they'd come. "If this doesn't work, we're going to have to shoot our way in."

"When have I ever led you astray?"

The soldier did have an exceptional record of quick thinking and creative solutions. At present, Kira was far more inclined to trust him than herself, even if the plan did sound a little crazy.

Kyle led them to a private office he'd identified, likely belonging to a security officer, which was equipped with a terminal that offered direct access into the security system. Getting past the firewall would take some work, but that wouldn't be a problem for the tech-savvy soldier.

"Give me a few minutes," Kyle said as he got settled at the workstation. He began pairing his suit with the console in anticipation of the sensor integration.

Kira kept an eye on her HUD while she waited. It still didn't seem right that there had only been guards at the entrance and they hadn't seen others since. Moreover, the stun effect of the sonic blasts would have worn off minutes before, yet there had been no general alarm. "What the fok is going on here?" she muttered to no one in particular.

"Is there anything Mysar offers over other worlds?" Nia asked.

"This planet's resources are a bigger topic than what's happening in this facility," Kira countered.

"Maybe not," the soldier continued. "If the aliens made a point of placing people in key positions of power within the government, maybe it was for some other end."

Kira considered the statement. "For the sake of argument, yes, Valta or Elusia are far more habitable worlds. Mysar is different in two ways—its people, and the amount of metals in its soil."

"What do you mean about the people?" Ari asked.

"The culture here," Kira continued. "It's more… aggressive than the other worlds in this system."

"Just like the neural chemistry in Kaen and Jared," Nia completed for her.

"When I was inside Kaen's mind, I sensed Nox's hunger. I didn't know for what at the time, but I'm beginning to think the aliens feed on—this is going to sound weird—negative emotional energy. After all, think about the TRs."

"It does sound a little weird," Nia agreed, "but too many observations are stacking up at this point. So, couple a chronically bitter population with an abundance of metals and that sounds like evil aliens ramping up their forces."

"Come to think of it, all those coded logs did indicate much higher-volume mining activity than would be expected for a population this size," Kyle interjected without looking up from his work at the desk.

"Mining Mysar and manipulating its people, but for what end?" Kira questioned.

"Expansion or war, most likely," Ari speculated.

All the pieces began falling into place in Kira's head. "The Gaelon System is close enough that it wouldn't take too much effort to transfer materials from Mysar to there. So, this could be just an outpost."

Nia crossed her arms. "Great, so taking out Hale might not even get us the real bad guys."

"Not entirely, but she'll likely have all the information we need to locate who she's working with," Kira said. "I never thought this would end with her."

"Good," Kyle cut in, "because she's not alone."

"You located Hale?" Kira rushed over to look at the monitor on the desk.

Kyle pointed to several dots on the facility layout, displaying the data that had been filtered through his suit's sensors. "She *is* up on the second level, but not exactly where we were headed. This section is walled off from the rest of the building and appears to have direct access to the underground levels."

Kira studied the layout. "Is that a doorway from the chancellor's chambers?" She indicated a break in the fortified wall.

"I think so," Kyle replied. "If we go in that way, we'll need to pass by two sets of guards. I suggest we go down and come up through here." He traced a path with his index finger along the screen.

"The access point in isn't too far from here," Kira observed.

"No, and now that I'm in the security system, I can block their ability to pick up any traces of our stealth suits." Kyle's voice hinted at a smile behind his opaque faceplate.

"You really are good." Kira smiled back.

"Don't stroke his ego," Nia cautioned.

"Oh, this is just praise for my unmitigated awesomeness," Kyle shot back. "Relevant architectural layouts and a real-time feed from the facility security system are being routed to your HUDs now."

Nia sighed. "Show off."

Once Kyle had returned the desk to look like how he'd found it, Kira motioned her team into the hall. She jogged toward the back entrance Kyle had identified.

Fifteen meters down the corridor, she heard approaching footfalls and the faint scuffing sound of tactical gear rubbing against body armor.

"I think those guards are finally awake and back after us," Kira warned her team.

"They can't see us," Kyle assured her. "As long as we don't physically run into them, we're as good as invisible."

"They can't have gone far!" one of the guards shouted down the hall. "They disappeared from the feed in the chief's office."

The voice was getting closer.

Kira halted her advance and pressed herself against the side wall. A moment later, a group of soldiers came around the nearby corner, headed straight for her.

"Never should have let them make it inside," another soldier grumbled.

"Their tech wasn't supposed to be this good," the first replied. "We're not just dealing with the Elusians anymore."

The six armored guards passed by, coming within half a meter of brushing against Kira. She kept her cool and waited until they were well past before she moved.

"Let's get to the chancellor's position," Kira told her team while she resumed the jog toward their destination.

Upon reaching the supposed back doorway to the stairwell, Kira was unable to see the entrance. "Is this it?" she asked Kyle.

"Yeah, must be a hidden panel," he replied. He walked back and forth twice in front of the location. "This part of the panel is definitely narrower." He ran his gloved hand over the surface.

"There have to be controls somewhere." Nia joined him in the search. "Ah! Here's an access port."

The two soldiers used their interface tools to hack into the door lock. After thirty seconds, the wall clicked, followed by a *hiss* as the panel swung inward.

"Well, so much for keeping our location secret," Ari said.

"I tried to block the security notice but no guarantees," Kyle said. "Better hurry."

They slipped through the opening, and Kira pressed the control next to the door to close the panel. The stairwell was unadorned, with cast concrete stairs and a metal railing. It extended down at least five stories, but the lights were off so Kira couldn't see the bottom. Their destination was the level above, so she sprinted up the stairs.

At the top, Ari took the lead, his gun drawn and ready. He peeked around the corner. "I see two guards at the access door," he reported. "No additional locks."

The visual confirmed what Kira saw on her HUD. "We'll need to get as close to the chancellor as possible without being seen. Once we have her in custody, we'll have a bartering chip for getting out of here."

"I see four guards inside with her," Kyle reported.

Nia hugged the side wall as she crept forward. "There are more in the anteroom."

"Take out the two soldiers outside with a sonic blast," Kira ordered.

"Aye." Ari fired off two rapid shots, and the guards dropped to the floor.

"Go!" Kira ran forward with her team. They took up positions on either side of the door. "Let's see if we can lure the others into the open." She tapped on the door with the butt of her handgun.

A moment later, the door cracked open and a guard stuck her head out. "Is everything—"

Kira shot her with a sonic blast.

The woman dropped to the ground in the threshold, forcing the door open the rest of the way.

"Oh, shite!" Kyle swore.

Kira's HUD updated. The room on the other side of the chancellor's chamber didn't have four soldiers, but a dozen.

"Shite, they must have been masked in the system and our suits couldn't read them through the walls," Kyle said.

"Okay, so shooting our way in was a bad idea," Kira realized.

Gentle footfalls approached the doorway, and Hale came into view. "If you attack me, Ellen dies."

Kira held up her hand for her team to remain motionless and silent.

"I know it's you, Kira. I can feel you." Hale stepped over the fallen guard's body.

How does she know me by name? Did Ellen tip her off? Kira slowed her breathing, even though she knew it wouldn't make a difference to the suit. Her heart pounded in her ears, and the chancellor stepped within a meter of her position, looking straight at her.

"Your mind is very powerful. It's a shame you won't use it to its full potential," the older woman stated. "Are you ready to embrace your new self, Kira?"

Kira swallowed. *I will never become the monster she wants me to be.*

A presence appeared in her mind. *"Ah, there you are!"*

Shite! Kira tried to block the alien, but she couldn't force it back.

"At last we meet, Kira. No need to be scared now."

In front of her, Hale smiled. "Perhaps you need some additional motivation. They're here!" she shouted.

Inside the meeting room, two more guards entered with Ellen. Her hair was mussed and her pantsuit was wrinkled, but otherwise she looked unharmed.

"If you value your associate's life, you will show yourselves," Hale stated. "I won't ask again."

Kira closed her eyes and took a slow breath. "We can't let

a civilian get hurt. Disable the stealth but don't disarm," she instructed her team over the internal comm.

She deactivated her own armor's stealth and then immediately said over the external speaker, "All right, Hale. Let's talk."

CHAPTER 21

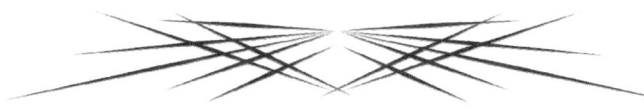

STANDING FACE-TO-FACE WITH the chancellor, Kira could feel the strength of the alien presence within her. Anyone other than a true telepath could easily mistake that power for the magnetism of a natural leader, but Kira knew better. There was more to this woman than just charisma.

Unfortunately, to learn more about the presence within, Kira couldn't play it safe. The being had allowed a temporary mental connection, but Kira had no chance of forcing her way into Hale's mind without an optical link.

She reached for the release on her helmet.

"What are you doing?" Nia hissed over the team's internal comms.

"To take out the alien, I need to get to Hale herself," Kira replied. "Telepathy is our only way out of this." She undid the helmet's latch and slipped it from her head.

A pleased smile touched the chancellor's lips. "Ah, so now we can really meet."

"I'm who you're really after. Let Ellen go," Kira demanded.

"So you can shoot all of us and leave? No." The chancellor

shook her head. "The only way your team is getting out of here is if you stop treating me like the enemy, Kira."

"Sorry, but holding civilians at gunpoint isn't really helping your case," Kira retorted.

"A necessity driven by your stubbornness. You say you are willing to hand yourself over in exchange for her, but you have no genuine intention of doing so."

It wouldn't take a telepath to know that much. No one who made that offer ever *really* meant it. The statement was a stall tactic. In any other negotiation, Kira might have been able to exert some small measure of telepathic influence to make the subject believe her. This time, whatever she said, the chancellor would see right through it.

Thinking back over her career, Kira realized it was rare for her to be truly open and honest with anyone. Careful word choice and omissions were a part of communication, conscious or not.

Now, though, she wouldn't have anything to hide behind. She would have to face the unshielded mind of this unknown enemy.

"Spoken words are never going to achieve a resolution to this standoff," Kira stated, looking directly at the chancellor.

"At last, some truth," the older woman replied. "Let us get to know one another."

A presence returned to Kira's mind. *"Such wasted potential. You can be so much more."*

"Who are you?" Kira replied, trying to trace her way back to the alien's mind. She could feel it in the distance, deep within Hale, but there was a wall around it.

"I am what allowed you to be."

"That's not an answer!" Kira shouted in her mind. *"You want to lead me, so show your true face."*

A mental image of a landscape appeared. Kira didn't recognize the world as any place she'd been, though the elements were familiar—forest over gently rolling hills, a lake, mountains in the distance. It could almost pass for Valta if it weren't for a chartreuse tint to the sky.

"What is this place?" Kira asked. *"This doesn't tell me who you are."*

"But it does," the presence replied. *"Open your mind."*

Hesitantly, Kira allowed herself to delve deeper into the image. What Kira had taken to be trees now looked strange to her. They were rooted in the ground and branched like the organic foliage she knew from her home, but these structures were too rigid. A breeze passed through, yet no branches swayed.

"These are mechanical," Kira observed.

"Not quite, but also not wood. It is our... home."

The mental image zoomed out, showing that the forest was arranged as a circle nestled within the valley. The trees formed an intricate pattern, almost like Kira was looking at circuitry. The forms were so familiar. She wracked her memory about where she'd seen the image—sometime recent.

"This is what we saw in Kaen's mind!" Kira exclaimed telepathically.

"Before, you saw the receiver. This is the transmitter."

"It's massive."

"One individual is easy to control."

A chill spread through Kira. *Their plan was always to build an army.*

And, of course, there would need to be a way to control that army. With the right control network, one individual couldn't only possess a remote target, a whole group could be under a single individual's command.

Kira swallowed. *"Why are you showing me this? Now I know what I need to destroy."*

"You will never reach it."

"When are you going to understand that you constantly underestimate us?"

The presence chuckled in her mind. *"We are far older than you, and we have the knowledge of dozens of lifetimes. It is you who underestimates us."*

Regardless of which side was mistaken—or both—Kira needed to get answers. She could reasonably guess the world she had been shown was in the Gaelon System, but that didn't explain what the beings were or how they operated. A biomechanical forest that doubled as a massive transmitter could point in a number of directions.

"Do you have bodies of your own?" Kira asked after a brief pause to collect her thoughts.

"Such simple vessels… so limiting," the presence replied.

"I'll take that as 'no'."

"Your vantage is so narrow for what it is to be an individual versus one of many. The vessels we will create will bring out the best of all forms."

The image of the forest faded from Kira's mind. *"So, you are one of many… and one in the same?"*

A sense of affirmation filled Kira's consciousness. *"A single individual can never compare to what we are."*

"But I met Nox. It spoke as an individual, just as I am speaking with you now."

"Distinctions are never so simple. Even now, Kira, don't you find yourself wondering where one ends and another begins?"

Kira's surroundings distorted—first a flash, and then everything began to stretch away from her. She became but a tiny speck amid a vast network of minds. The powerful consciousness around her bore down, forcing her back into herself.

"You still think you can stand up to us?" the presence bellowed inside her.

Kira cowered within herself, unprepared to face a consciousness of that magnitude.

"Even a fraction of one of us can overtake you," it sneered. *"You will be our tool."*

The presence closed around Kira's mind, gripping her in the way it had taken over Kaen, Hale, Jared, and stars knew how many others. It had her trapped, and it knew it.

No. I'm more than this.

Kira stood her ground, forcing the entity back to the edges of her mind. She was still confined, but she was far from consumed. *"Is that all you have?"*

She drove her own telepathic spear into the alien consciousness, looking for clues about who it was and how she could manipulate it.

The walls Kira had detected around the enemy mind were cracking. She forced mental spears through the weak points while taking as much care as she could to not cause permanent damage. Hale—the real Hale—was in there somewhere, and she had to find her.

Once inside, Kira began stripping away layers of consciousness, sorting the thoughts and feelings of the possessing entity versus the native mind. However, much to her distress, she found all of the recent thoughts had originated from the alien. Hale was nowhere to be found.

"Where are you?" Kira called out as she dug deeper. She received no reply.

But even though Hale was missing, Kira detected the core of the other consciousness. *"Ah, there you are!"*

The alien swelled in response to her direct contact, making itself appear as large as possible within its host. *"This is only a part of me. You won't be able to drive me away."*

"She's not yours to control. Leave!"

"She has been mine for longer than she ever was herself. Do not meddle in what you don't understand."

Kira's heart leaped. *"How long has it been?"*

The alien ignored her. *"You are no closer to leaving here with your colleagues, Kira. Admit my superiority and I will consider letting them go."*

"After you've shown me what you are? There's no way I can ever trust you."

"Then I will make you."

Kira was thrust back from the chancellor's mind in an instant. A high-pitched scream rattled in her skull, seemingly coming from everywhere at once. The vibration seeped into her, crawling under her skin and burrowing deep within. The deeper it went, the stronger the scream became, until the vibrations became so intense it felt like physical bonds threaded through her.

They snaked their way upward and embedded in her mind, burning their way to their destination.

A fire ignited behind Kira's eyes, searing her nerves as the burn radiated down her arms and legs.

The scream warped into a deafening buzz that overwhelmed Kira's hearing. Her vision closed in around her. She had no sense of place or purpose, only rage welling within.

Kill. Destroy. Make them suffer.

She wasn't sure if the thoughts were her own or were being projected into her mind.

Show them what you are now.

She was hungry, so very hungry, to feel the others' pain—

to drown out her own.

Her vision all but red, she rounded on the faceless forms around her. They stood in her way, but they wouldn't for long.

— — —

The guards to either side of Ellen froze with fear. They raised their kinetic weapons, but their fingers twitched on the triggers, as though held back from firing by some unseen force.

Ellen stumbled backward away from them. *What the...?*

In front of her, Kira writhed in apparent agony. A snarl escaped her lips, revealing metallic fangs growing from her mouth. Her exposed skin took on a scaly appearance, transitioning into armored plates covering her hair and wrapping back over her head.

What the fok is happening?! Ellen's back hit the wall. She shimmied sideways, not taking her eyes from Kira.

A mere three meters away, the woman she'd known since childhood was unrecognizable. Metallic scales now extended down her neck. Fifteen-centimeter talons pierced the fingertips of her gloves.

The creature's luminescent orange eyes fixed on Ellen's position.

"This can't be you, Kira," Ellen murmured.

She couldn't process what she was seeing. And alien? A Taran-engineered monster? It must be connected to what the Guard was investigating at MTech—the 'Robus' that Hale had mentioned earlier. But how had they gotten to Kira?

"Get down!" a man shouted at her.

Ellen ducked just in time to miss a sonic blast from one of the Guard soldier's multi-handguns as it rippled through the air. The two guards who had escorted her into the room dropped to the floor.

Dazed, Ellen turned to see another of the Guard soldiers advancing, his multi-handgun trained on Kira.

"Wh—what's going on?" Ellen stammered. "Is she a… Robus?"

"Where did you hear that term?"

"From Hale. How did—"

"We'll explain later," the man said. "I'm Ari, one of Kira's team members. Get behind me."

Ellen tried to suppress her fear as she scrambled behind the large, armored soldier. She positioned herself between the wall and Ari, her back toward the corner.

Kira pivoted to follow Ellen's movements. She kept her distance from Ari, but she bared her fangs in aggression.

"Is she going to kill us?" Ellen asked.

"Certainly looks like she wants to." Ari raised his weapon with one hand and reached into a compartment on his suit with another. "But we won't let that happen."

He took a step forward. "Kira, if you can hear me in there, you need to get ahold of yourself."

"That's not going to work," a female soldier said, coming up next to him. "She lost herself this time."

Ari produced a compact syringe from the compartment in his armor. "Help me subdue her, Nia."

The Kira-Robus leaped back from them, spinning toward a cluster of the frozen Mysaran soldiers. She closed the distance in a split second, moving so quickly it almost looked like she'd skipped through space. Before Ellen could blink, the creature had backhanded the soldiers, knocking them to the ground, unconscious.

The female soldier took a sharp breath. "Was that coincidence, or…?"

A second later, the Kira-Robus rounded on Chancellor Hale, staring straight into her eyes.

Ari shook his head with disbelief. "Stars, it *is* still her!" He looked at the syringe in his hand. "I think we can find a better use for this."

His companion nodded.

The two soldiers ran toward the chancellor, leaving Ellen alone by the wall. She looked on as they and their third soldier companion converged on Hale. Ari thrust the syringe into the chancellor's jugular and emptied the contents.

Hale swayed on her feet for a moment before falling flat on her back.

Narrowing its orange eyes, the Kira-Robus stepped forward to stand over the chancellor, one leg to either side of her hips. She stared down at the prone woman. "No more games."

CHAPTER 22

KIRA KNEW SHE wasn't herself, but she swore to control the rage that had overcome her only moments before. It didn't need to be channeled toward destruction. Instead, she could use it for power.

I am stronger than the darkness, she told herself. *Its presence doesn't change who I am.*

Though others the aliens had encountered may have been easily swayed, Kira sensed that she was different. She recognized how the gifts she had possessed since birth were a byproduct of these aliens. That linked her to them, in a way. They couldn't fully possess her because she was already one of them.

The realization came to her slowly as she grazed the surface of the chancellor's mind. The answers were locked away, just out of reach. She had to find them, so she could not only get in touch with her new self but also save the innocents she had sworn to protect.

As she stood over the chancellor's incapacitated form, Kira knew appearances were deceiving. Inside the chancellor's body, a consciousness was very much awake. And it was time to talk.

Kira snapped a mental cage around the presence within. *"Who are you?"* she demanded.

This time, the alien was caught off-guard by not having the upper hand. *"You may call me Reya,"* it replied.

"All right, Reya. What the fok do you want?"

"What we have always wanted—to grow stronger."

Kira tightened her mental restraints. *"Well, time to rethink your strategies. You've messed with the wrong people this time."*

"The plans are already in motion. Eliminating me won't change a thing."

"It'll get you off this planet and out of the mind of this innocent woman. I'll count that as a win."

The alien gave a mental sigh. *"It's not that simple, Kira. You know it's not just me."*

Kira felt a tug on invisible tethers extending from Hale. In her mind's eye, she saw the network throughout the Mysaran government—dozens of hosts for this Reya presence, or its as-yet-unseen associates, to possess at will. Connected to that network was also the head of MTech.

It all linked back to Hale. She was the foundation of the conduit leading back to the alien base a system away. If that conduit could be severed...

How do I cut the connection without hurting the host? Kira knew she'd need Leon and Doctor Elric to dissolve the TR in the woman's brain, but perhaps a telepathic block would be possible as a short-term solution. If Kira could locate Hale within, she'd have an ally to suppress the alien presence through a simultaneous assault on two fronts.

She dove through the alien's consciousness, searching for pathways into what lay underneath.

"What are you doing, Kira?" Reya questioned, a hint of concern slipping into its mental tone.

"I already told you that you don't belong here," Kira replied. *"I'm going to get you out."*

"I know what you're trying to do, but you won't like what you find," Reya cautioned.

"I'll take my chances."

Kira dove deeper, stripping away layers of tangled memories. *I know she's in here somewhere.*

Reya tried to block Kira's search, though all the barriers were easily overcome. Kira was in control—if only temporarily—and she had a mission to complete.

In time, she found herself deeper inside the chancellor's mind than she'd ever ventured in another. Raw emotion flooded through her. Pain and suffering—the fuel Reya and its kind so desperately desired. Reya had had its own power source buried within, as Cynthia Hale had remained trapped inside herself, suffering. The greatest torture of all was to have witnessed decades of abuse perpetrated by her own hands. Hands she couldn't control.

There, in the deepest depths of her mind, Cynthia still looked on with horror.

"Chancellor!" Kira exclaimed, rushing toward the mental form of the weary woman.

"That isn't me," came a weak reply.

"It's okay, ma'am. We're going to bring you back to our lab and get it out of you."

The mental projection of the woman looked up at Kira. *"It will never be gone. It's been in me for too long."*

"That's not true. You're still here. That means there's more than enough left to save."

"No, you don't understand." Cynthia shuddered. *"I*

wouldn't even have a life to go back to."

"You can always start over," Kira tried to assure her.

"No. I'm just a remnant, an echo of what was. I died when it took me over."

Kira recoiled from the woman's bitterness. Never had she felt such darkness and defeat. *"I… We can find a way to help you."*

"If you want to help me, then let me die," Cynthia pleaded. *"Please, kill me!"*

Kira pulled back further as the woman clawed at her. *"Make it end! Kill me! I can't live in this prison any longer!"*

Her moans filled Kira's consciousness, begging for death to release her.

Memories of the time spent imprisoned in her own mind swirled around Kira, offering scattered glimpses into a lifetime of lies. She had been so young when Reya took her, no more than twenty years old. Ambitious and bright, she was the perfect host to manipulate toward gaining ultimate control.

Cynthia hadn't wanted that life. She had always hoped for peace in her home system, and to unite. To have watched for decades as her alien possessor tried to tear the system apart had destroyed her every day.

All feeling, all sense of hope had been stripped away. This tiny nugget was all that remained of her former self—an ember reignited for one brief moment before it was to be extinguished forever. And she was begging for Kira's help to finally do something on her own terms.

"I can't kill you," Kira told her with a heavy heart. *"I can't give you what you ask."*

"No, please! You'll never be able to get Reya out. Some of it will always be stuck here, eating away. I can't go on like this. There's nothing left for me."

"*I'm sworn to protect.*"

"*Then protect me from this monster.*"

Even if Kira could stomach killing an innocent for their own long-term wellbeing, she couldn't be responsible for the execution of a foreign head of state. Personal beliefs aside, that wasn't a decision she could make on the Taran Empire's behalf.

"*We're going to get you back to our Guard base, and they'll—*"

Cynthia sobbed in her mind. "*No more prisons. Let it end.*"

Kira was crippled by indecision. She felt the woman's suffering as if it were her own, and she understood the wish for death. Were the roles reversed, she'd want it for herself.

As she assessed Cynthia's state, Kira was astonished to see how far the alien had embedded in her. It wasn't just one localized place in her brain, but a series of foreign structures integrated throughout her body. Her entire nervous system was affected. Even if it was possible for Doctor Elric and Leon to flush the alien presence from her body and make it so it couldn't come back, Cynthia's original organics had withered. The damage was done. They might be able to restore her mind, but the best prognosis would be to remain a prisoner in a useless body.

"*I have nothing to live for,*" Cynthia murmured. "*No friends, no family that is my own. I want it to end.*"

Kira wished she could make the woman's suffering go away, to take back the decades of torture. She could rid them from her mind, but that would be no better than what Reya had done.

One thing was certain: Kira couldn't do nothing. She made up her mind.

"*I can't kill you, but I can give you a few moments of yourself,*" Kira said.

Cynthia nodded in her mind. *"Thank you. When I'm gone, stop them."*

"I will."

Kira kept a mental tether on Cynthia as she withdrew from her mind. Around her, the three members of her team stood with their weapons drawn, watching intently. Ellen was still crouched in the corner with an expression of terrified fascination. Kira looked at her hands and saw she had returned to her normal form.

"I need you to turn around," Kira told her team.

"Ma'am—" Ari started to object.

"That's an order," she stated.

Reluctantly, the three soldiers turned their backs to her.

Kira stared into the chancellor's eyes, tracing the tether back to Cynthia within. *"Be free."*

The chancellor shuddered and then gasped. Her eyes went wide and wild, fighting through the sedative. "I'm—!" She rolled to her side and crawled toward a disabled soldier two meters from her. Hands shaking, she grabbed a utility knife from the soldier's hip pouch. She looked toward Kira. "Thank you." Cynthia drew the blade across her throat.

Kira squeezed her eyes shut and turned away.

"What the fok?" Kyle exclaimed.

"Holy shite." Nia sucked in a deep breath.

Ari's eyes searched hers. "What did you do?"

"I freed her," she replied. "I gave her a few moments as herself. That's what she wanted."

Ari lowered his weapon. "We were supposed to bring her back for questioning!"

"She'd suffered enough."

A pool of blood formed around Cynthia's body as the life faded from her.

Kira swallowed. "We should—"

Choking moans sounded around the room, and half of the guards spasmed on the floor. Five seconds later, they became still, and their eyes slowly opened.

"What happened?" one murmured.

"Where am I?" another asked.

The one closest to Kira, whose knife Cynthia has taken, reached for his gun. "Who are you?" He spotted the chancellor's corpse. "The fok?"

Kira's soldiers hurriedly put on their helmets and reactivated their suits' stealth mode.

She located her own helmet several paces away and made a run for it. She dove the last two paces as one of the guards fired. The blast barely missed her shoulder.

Kira hit the ground and rolled to the side, sliding her helmet over her head in one smooth motion. She activated the stealth tech.

The guards grunted with momentary confusion but then began tracing her likely path.

On her HUD, Kira saw the members of her team darting for Ellen's position.

Ari was the first to reach her. He grabbed her hand and pulled her to her feet.

Ellen recoiled from the cold, invisible touch at first, then realization passed over her face. She followed his directions toward the door.

Kira fired a warning kinetic shot into the ceiling with her multi-handgun, then switched back to sonic mode. "Don't follow us." She shot off three sonic blasts around the room, hoping to hit as many guards as possible with the wide spread.

Kira's soldiers were headed for the back door.

"No," Ellen stopped them. "Out this way." She pointed for

the door through which the guards had entered.

"That'll lead out to the landing above the main lobby," Kyle objected.

"Which gives us the straightest shot to outside. Trust me." Ellen jogged ahead.

Kira followed. "Come on!"

The adjacent room was empty, since all of the guards had entered the meeting room when the conflict began. Kira ran to the door on the right wall, which her HUD indicated led to the lobby. She tried the door handle. Locked.

There was no time to crack the security. Kira pulled her rifle from her back and started shooting. The lock exploded in a satisfying spray of melted shrapnel.

"That's one way to open a door." She kicked her armored boot against the pulverized surface and it flew open. She holstered the rifle.

Cries of surprise sounded from downstairs. Kira spotted the open stairwell to her left. At the top, two guards had their weapons leveled in her direction. Thanks to the stealth armor, her exact position was invisible.

Kira held up her hand to stop her team from coming through the opening. She fired a sonic blast with her multi-handgun at the guards, and they crumpled to the floor.

"All right, there are mostly civilians downstairs, but more guards are certainly on their way," she said to her team. "Ellen, you're an escaping worker—pretend we aren't here. Move quickly." She headed down the stairs.

"What just happened in there?" Nia asked over the suit's interior comm, following Kira down.

"Those soldiers and head of MTech were linked to Hale," Kira explained. "When she died, the alien no longer had a host to support its telepathic link."

"But Nox jumped from Kaen into Jared."

"Nox wasn't embedded like Reya here—that was this one's name. It was too large and complex to go into someone else. Nox was like an infant by comparison."

"Foking fantastic," Kyle muttered.

When they reached the switch-back landing on the stairway, Kira paused to make sure no one was about to try to blow their heads off. Fortunately, the lobby's occupants appeared to have scattered when they heard gunfire upstairs.

"Okay, at the bottom, we head through those doors," she pointed, following the indicators on her HUD, "and then it's a relatively straight shot out the front door."

"Should I have the shuttle meet us around this side of the building?" Kyle asked.

Kira nodded. "Do it." She noticed a new proximity alert flash across her vision. "And bring it close. I imagine we'll be under fire on our way out."

The rest of her team noticed the alert on their own HUDs.

"I'm on it!" Kyle bolted down the stairs.

Nia positioned herself between Ellen and the incoming enemy, weapon raised. While Ellen would still be visible, Nia's armor would at least protect her.

"Go for the door. I'll hold them off," Kira instructed.

They descended the final steps, and Kira crouched behind the base support column. Her team ran across the lobby, passing through the door a second before the first guards came into view.

"Target detected through—" The guard never got the chance to finish his statement.

Kira lobbed a flash grenade, followed by a burst of sonic blasts.

The soldiers stopped their advance for a moment, but as

the scene cleared following the grenade, it was obvious they were still standing.

Shite, they must have muted their external comm mics. Kira judged the distance to the exit doorway. It wasn't far; she could make it in a sprint.

"Someone is still here!" one guard shouted. He tossed a smoke grenade into the center of the room.

Kira bit back a curse as the fine smoke spread. Her suit was great at making her blend in with the surroundings, but having anything like smoke in the air would result in a big soldier-shaped hole.

She had a split second to act. With no other choice, she ran for the door. Though her suit did its best to mask her movement, the air was already too thick with debris, and she was running too hard for her suit to mask her footfalls.

The first volley of kinetic shots hit the back of her armor a meter from the doorway. She raced through and slammed the door closed behind her.

Her team was pressed against the side walls of the corridor.

Ari looked at his chest plate, which had been sticking out just enough to deflect a bullet and keep Ellen from taking a shot to her head.

The woman's breath was ragged as she realized what had just happened. "Oh, shite."

"Yeah. These friends of yours aren't very nice," Kira said. "This door won't hold, come on!"

They took off at full speed. Ellen began to fall behind, so Ari scooped her into his arms.

Kira would have previously been winded by the sprint, but she found she was easily able to keep up with her team as they made the final push toward the exit.

A door smashed open somewhere behind them, but she

didn't bother to look. More guards were no doubt coming, and they'd keep coming so long as there was anyone left standing.

"Home stretch!" Nia cheered.

Kira could see the way to the side exit on her HUD. Unfortunately, there was also a line of Mysaran guards blocking their path ahead.

"Fok!" Nia exclaimed. "Sonic blasts aren't viable in that configuration."

They couldn't make a run for it, either, without getting too holey for Kira's liking.

"The shuttle will be here in one minute. If it sets down out there, they'll blow it up and we'll be *really* stuck," Kyle cautioned.

"Are you still patched into the security system?" Kira asked him.

"Yeah, but I'm pretty sure they know we're right foking here."

"Can you feed sonic feedback through their comms?"

Kyle considered her suggestion. "I can try." He made some rapid entries on his mobile tablet. "If this works, we'll know right about—"

The soldiers in the lobby simultaneously raised their hands to their ears, trying to rip out their comms.

"Go!" Kira shouted.

Her team raced across the open lobby while the guards were temporarily distracted. Nia shot out the door lock and busted it open with her shoulder to clear a path for the others.

Twenty meters from the building's exit, their shuttle was on final descent to the dusty ground.

They closed the remaining distance in a mad dash amid kinetic rounds, with Ari shielding Ellen against his chest.

The group piled into the shuttle, and Kira hit the back

hatch controls. Kyle ran to the front of the craft with Nia. The shuttle lifted from the ground and rocketed toward space.

Kira collapsed into one of the passenger chairs and removed her helmet. "That was way too close."

Ari lowered Ellen from his shoulder, and she slumped into a chair across from Kira.

"Thank you for getting me out of there," Ellen murmured. "I'm so sorry. I was only trying to help."

"Next time, leave it to the professionals." Kira fluffed her red hair with her fingers.

The other woman paused. "What happened to you?"

"That's a long, classified story," Kira said. "But, given what you've seen, I suspect a debrief is in order. That approval will need to come from higher up the command chain."

Ellen took a shaky breath, still clearly in shock. "Is the chancellor really dead?"

Kira gave a solemn nod. "Her body, anyway. As for the thing that was controlling her, I suspect it's gone rather than dead—that its consciousness went back to… wherever it came from. The others it had its telepathic tendrils in are themselves again."

Ellen nodded.

"Politics you can do, stick to that. No more action hero business," Kira advised.

"Yeah." Ellen cracked a smile. "I don't think I'll be leaving my office any time soon."

"Approaching the *Raven*," Kyle stated from the cockpit.

Kira took a slow breath. "This will be another fun mission brief to write."

Ellen gave a sheepish look to the team. "I don't suppose I could get a ride home?"

CHAPTER 23

LEON HELD KIRA in a quiet embrace. "Are you sure you're okay?" he asked her again.

"Yes, I'm fine." She beamed at him. "I feel better than I have all week."

He released a long breath. "Okay."

Her account of the events on Mysar had been alarming, to say the least, but he knew that he'd better get used to her harrowing tales of near-death. In all fairness, he'd been shot at multiple times that week, too. *The era of being a lab jockey is officially over.*

Leon released Kira from the hug and looked her over again. "I still don't know what to make of Hale—of one being controlling that many people."

Kira leaned against the hallway wall in the Orion Station's science wing. "It was *in* her, not just possessing her." She looked down. "I wish we'd been able to recover her body for you to examine."

"Part of me is relieved."

"Yeah, I wouldn't want to do that autopsy, either." Kira

wiped her hands down her face. "Hey, has Jared been through the extraction yet?"

Leon shook his head. "Elric was running one more round of tests before we do. Our time to work with him is up in a couple of hours."

Kira got a glint in her eyes. "You know that world I told you about, the one Reya showed me?"

"Yeah."

"What if we could find it?"

Leon frowned. "Somewhere in Gaelon, right?"

"But systems are huge, and we have no idea how many planets there are or how large those planets may be. What if we could locate the exact position of that forest that was sending the telepathic commands?"

"I don't like where this is going." Leon crossed his arms. *If she knows that exact location, she'll almost certainly try to go there.*

"If we don't take them out, then what happened to Mysar could happen somewhere else."

"Yes, if your assumptions are correct, in theory it would be possible to locate the source of the signal," Leon yielded.

"Then let's find it." Kira grinned.

"You should pull in Sandren and Kaen," Leon suggested. "I'm not sure what kind of record we'll be able to make of the location." If they needed to authorize a mission later, it was best that they witness the mysterious intel firsthand.

"Yes, good call."

"Not that I think you should be the one to go on said mission, considering the aliens' fixation on you."

She flashed a sweet smile. "I like knowing that you care."

While walking back toward Leon's lab, Kira sent the two commanding officers a message about what they had planned, and they replied with affirmation that they'd come to meet them.

Doctor Elric, Jack, Tess were working in the lab when Leon and Kira arrived. Jared was strapped to a mobile medical bed, in a drug-induced half-sleep. Two soldiers stood guard over him.

"Oh, Kira. Good, you're back," Doctor Elric stated. "I was hoping to get your help with some final testing."

"Would this, by chance, have to do with measuring what happens to the TR in Jared's brain while Nox is active?" she asked.

The doctor looked surprised. "How did you know?

"Because I had a similar thought. I'd like to see if we can isolate the specific telepathic frequency, or electromagnetic signature, or whatever that resonates with the TR in Jared's brain so we can use it to search for the transmitter."

"A strategy I fully endorse," Colonel Kaen said from behind her. He was standing near the doorway alongside Major Sandren.

"Sirs," Leon greeted.

"We're here as observers," Sandren said. "Please, go on."

"Do you think it's possible?" Kira asked Elric.

He nodded. "Isolate the signal in the TR? Certainly. I would have collected the data already, but I haven't been able to coax Nox to the forefront so I can take accurate measurements."

"I'd be happy to help with that," Kira said.

Doctor Elric and Jack made the necessary preparations to record Jared's brain activity. When they were finished, Elric indicated for Kira to proceed.

"All right, I'll get Nox talking," she said.

Leon watched as she bent over to look into Jared's eyes.

The captive went rigid under her intense gaze.

"Where are you?" Kira said in the tone Leon had come to associate with a telepathic command.

"Definitely getting something here," Elric said, looking over the readings on a monitor next to the bed. "We'll need a little more to get it fully calibrated."

"I've seen the world," Kira continued in her commanding tone. "Show me where it is." She leaned in. "I can feel you, Nox. You're trying to run." Her eyes narrowed. "Show me!"

Leon watched the struggle on Jared's face as Kira focused on Nox.

Elric kept a close eye on the monitor as the sensors continued processing inputs. "Isolating the signal now..."

"That's right, Nox," Kira said, her gaze intent. "You can't hide any longer."

"Okay, I think we have it," Doctor Elric announced. "Hopefully this data will be enough to help focus your scans."

"We'll begin searching the Gaelon System right away," Kaen acknowledged. "Now, I suggest you dissolve Jared's TR and sever Nox's connection for good."

— — —

Ellen sat down in the visitor chair under the watchful gaze of President Joris.

"Okay, so that could have gone better," she stated the obvious.

Joris leaned back in his chair, fingers steepled. "When I agreed to you going to Mysar, I thought it was to help the chancellor, not instigate her death."

"I know, sir, but she died years ago. This was a necessary tragedy."

He nodded. "A chance at a new beginning for us, indeed." He paused. "I think you should participate in discussions with the new heads of state."

"I had a hand in their previous leader's death. I'm not sure how well that would go over."

"That's not in the official record," Joris pointed out. "You know what really went on there before. That insight will be valuable when it comes to instituting a structure to keep this from happening again."

Ellen shifted in her chair. "Have any new Mysaran representatives been nominated yet?" she asked.

"No, but I heard it's in the works. MTech and several other companies are also going through a reorganization now that the alien influence is no longer present."

"Did they get a final count on the number of people who'd been subverted?"

"Over one hundred, in one capacity or another. They're rolling out a program to test for the TR your brother's team identified."

Ellen released a sigh of relief. "With that resolved, we can finally move forward."

"Indeed. Now that circumstances surrounding Mysar's opposition to rejoining the Empire have come to light, the matter has been reopened." Joris cracked a smile.

"Finally, a chance for peace."

"It's what we've all wanted, isn't it? Even if we went about it in different ways."

Ellen slumped back in her chair. "I can't believe the things I was willing to do for the Sovereign."

Joris' smile broadened. "Impressionable youth."

"And so horribly misguided. There's such a huge difference between cultural identity and autonomy. They aren't mutually exclusive."

"Our little Elvar Trinary will find our voice, I have no worries," the president replied. "We will remain Elusia, and hopefully Mysar can reestablish itself in a new image for the future."

"I *would* like to be a part of that, sir, if they'll have me."

"I'll make the suggestion as soon as it's appropriate. You're one of the few who've touched all three worlds in this system in a meaningful way—lived on each, knows the quirks and preferences. That will go a long way toward opening a productive dialogue."

Ellen smiled. "I look forward to being of service."

Joris nodded. "We have a long road ahead yet, but now we're on the right path."

— — —

Kira swiveled back and forth on a stool in Leon's office. The others had departed for the night, and most of the equipment had been shut down. She looked Leon over in the subtle blue glow cast from a screen.

"What aren't you saying?" she asked him.

He'd been distracted since her return from Mysar, but he had yet to make a clear indication as to why.

"Elric and I spent some time looking into your condition while you were away," he said at last.

"Right, that." Since her more controlled transformation on Mysar, she felt a new sense of confidence in the abilities, at least insomuch as she wasn't going to accidentally kill her loved ones. The agony she'd felt during the recent transformations, though… that was a problem.

"I have good news and bad," Leon continued.

"You know me. Always the bad first."

He nodded. "To put it bluntly, I don't think we can remove the nanites from you."

Kira's heart skipped a beat. She'd suspected as much, but part of her had been holding out hope that she could be free of the modification entirely. It was a much easier decision to walk away than to decide if she should take advantage of enhancements that were so unpredictable and painful.

"What are my options?" she asked, trying to remain objective.

"Well, though we can't remove the nanites, it might be possible to deactivate them."

"Would I go back to how I was before, then?"

He drummed his fingers on the countertop. "I'm honestly not sure. I ran a model using the equipment we got from the MTech lab, and the results were inconclusive."

"So, I'll be a freak for life." She sighed.

"But you'll be *my* freak." Leon smiled at her.

"You'll still love me when I have fangs and claws?"

He chuckled. "Well, I might have to kiss you more carefully under those conditions, but yes," he stepped forward and stroked the side of her face, "I'm in this with you. It doesn't change a thing."

Kira pulled him in for a hug and leaned her head against his chest. "I'm glad I don't have to go through this alone."

He held her close. "You'll never have to again."

After a minute of quiet reflection, Kira pulled away. "How would this suppressant thing work?"

Leon walked across the lab and grabbed a vial from a rack. "I don't know how effective this will be. It's just a first attempt. It'd be administered through a standard shot."

Kira nodded. "One time or ongoing?"

"Depends on how you respond," he replied. "There is another option. You could be paired with an AI."

She wasn't sure if the suggestion was just Leon spit-balling or if he'd talked with the Guard's leadership about it already. True AI pairs were relatively uncommon, especially on the core Taran worlds. While certain Taran planets had adopted a more tech-saturated culture, the current Taran vogue was to keep bodies in a more natural state. Having an implanted AI would make Kira even more of an outsider than she was already.

"I don't know." She crossed her arms. "It might be a little much to have another voice in my head on top of the whole telepathy thing."

"I don't doubt it, but an AI could help regulate you—probably a whole lot better than the suppressant we came up with."

Kira nodded. "Yeah, maybe. What would you do in my position?"

"I haven't felt what you've felt. It's not my place to say."

"From a medically objective standpoint, then," she prompted.

He sighed and leaned against the counter, facing her. "If I suddenly had super-strength and speed, I think I'd want to learn to master those abilities, even if it was painful. Those kinds of skills could come in handy. If an AI could help you achieve that, it's worth serious consideration."

"I'm glad to know there are options."

"I'll support you, no matter what you decide."

She took her free hand and drew him in for a kiss. "Those decisions can wait."

— — —

Kaen leaned back in his office chair. He was almost back to his usual routine, but there was still the unresolved issue of the alien threat.

It wasn't the Empire's way to wipe out an entire race without exhausting every other option—especially not under the new High Dynasty leadership. While the aliens' possession of autonomous individuals was heinous by Taran standards, the alien beings had their own perspective. If they could open a dialogue, perhaps there was still a chance the two races could find common ground. If not, they would take appropriate action.

A knock sounded on Kaen's office door.

"Come in, Major," he greeted Sandren. "Thank you for joining me."

"Of course, sir. What was it you wanted to discuss?"

Kaen steepled his fingers. "Now that we've identified the source of the alien signal, Guard command has authorized a recon mission to get a lay of the land."

"Kira's team?" Sandren prompted.

"Do you think she's ready to be back in the field?"

Sandren let out a long breath between his teeth. "She's not her old self, but she's been cleared by Medical."

"What about your gut instinct?"

The major folded his hands in his lap. "Given what we're up against, I think she's the only person for the job."

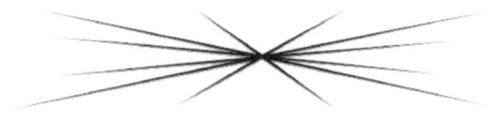

THE STORY CONTINUES IN *OFFENSIVE…*

Some missions need a personal touch.

After learning a race of telepathic aliens was behind her transformation into a Robus, Captain Kira Elsar wants answers. As the only person to have successfully communicated with the aliens, Kira is the best person to learn their enemy's true intentions.

The aliens are gearing up for a sinister power play, and Kira's home system—the Elvar Trinary—is ground zero. Kira must try to get inside the mind of the enemy to stop the attack before it begins. Except, Kira is part of the aliens' master plan, and every action she takes may be playing directly into their hands.

ALSO BY A.K. DUBOFF

Mindspace Series
Book 1: Infiltration
Book 2: Conspiracy
Book 3: Offensive
Book 4: Endgame

Cadicle Space Opera Series
Book 1: Rumors of War (Vol. 1-3)
Book 2: Web of Truth (Vol. 4)
Book 3: Crossroads of Fate (Vol. 5)
Book 4: Path of Justice (Vol. 6)
Book 5: Scions of Change (Vol. 7)

Dark Stars Trilogy
Book 1: Crystalline Space
Book 2: A Light in the Dark
Book 3: Masters of Fate

Troubled Space
Vol. 1: Brewing Trouble
Vol. 2: Stealing Trouble
Vol. 3: Making Trouble

AUTHOR'S NOTES

Thank you for coming on this journey through the Mindspace series with me! I can't express how much it means to have your support.

When I set out to write this series, I wanted to delve into a part of the Cadicle universe that wasn't addressed much in the original series—namely, the Tararian Guard and what goes on in the outer Taran colonies. I found myself wondering about other advanced races that might be lurking beyond the Taran sphere.

These thoughts eventually led me to the perennial concept of a scavenger race that absorbs others' tech and repurposes it for their own ends. There are classic examples of this in other sci-fi, such as the Borg in *Star Trek* or the Replicators in *Stargate*, but I found myself leaning in a slightly different direction for this alien foe. I wanted something that would push the boundaries of how we tend to think of life and get away from a being in its own mobile body.

If you've read the original Cadicle series, you know I tend to wander into the metaphysical with my writing. I spend a good deal of time in that series on telepathy, telekinesis, and astral projection. Maybe it's because I was a psychology major, as well as being the daughter of a psychologist, but I can nerd out for hours thinking and talking about the mind and how it relates to physical form.

So, the idea of Nox and its kind began to take shape—a race curious about physical experience but not autonomous beings unto themselves. It's a new challenge to have an enemy that one can't readily see or put in any one place. With a character like Kira and her unique skills, it only seemed appropriate for her to face an adversary that complemented her exploration of consciousness.

At any rate, that's a little backstory about how Mindspace came into being. I'm thrilled you're reading it, and I hope you're enjoying the ride!

Special thanks to Craig, Jim, John, Kurt, Tracey, Leo, Eric, Randy, Nick, Curtis, and Ron for beta reading and making sure I was doing the story justice. Thank you again to Andrew Dobell for the awesome cover and my tireless proofing team for spotting everything I miss. There's an old adage that writing is a solitary endeavor, but this amazing community has proved otherwise.

Stay tuned for *Mindspace: Offensive* as Kira's story continues!

ABOUT THE AUTHOR

A.K. (Amy) DuBoff has always loved science fiction in all its forms—books, movies, shows and games. If it involves outer space, even better!

Now a full-time author, Amy can frequently be found traveling the world. When she's not writing, she enjoys wine tasting, binge-watching TV series, and playing epic strategy board games.

To learn more or connect, visit www.amyduboff.com.